"We've been here before," Kelly said.

Jace stepped back and reached down to help her. "Yes, we have."

As she stood, her hands went to his shoulders and his caught her around the waist. Jace didn't release her immediately. Kelly looked up at him, her hands still on his shoulders.

"And we decided you wouldn't confuse me."

"Not we," he said. "You decided."

Jace drew her closer to him. His head dipped and he kissed her. She didn't try to stop him. His mouth was sweet on hers. It had been a long time since someone had held her like this. In his arms, Kelly felt safe. She let herself relax.

She would let herself enjoy the special moment, for now.

Dear Reader,

Kendall Farm is close to my heart. The place is fictitious, but in my mind it's as real as my own home. Like our heroine, Kelly, I know every inch of the farm and the grounds. Jace's family has owned it for generations. He popped into my consciousness, riding on horseback, and insisted that I tell his story. He hasn't had a wonderful life, but now he has an adopted son, Ari, and he's willing to sacrifice everything for the child.

Coming home to Kendall Farm, and discovering the place has been sold and the new owner is refusing to return it to the family, Jace can think of nothing except running. But not this time. This time he finds something worth staying for.

Happy endings,

Shirley Hailstock

HEARTWARMING

Summer on Kendall Farm

———

Shirley Hailstock

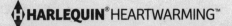

Recycling programs
for this product may
not exist in your area.

ISBN-13: 978-0-373-36710-8

Summer on Kendall Farm

Copyright © 2015 by Shirley Hailstock

Printed in U.S.A.

www.Harlequin.com

Shirley Hailstock began her writing life as a lover of reading. She likes nothing better than to find a quiet corner where she can get lost in a book, explore new worlds and visit places she never expected to see. As an author, she can not only visit those places, but she can be the heroine of her own stories. The author of over thirty novels and novellas, including her electronic editions, Shirley has received numerous awards, including the Waldenbooks Bestselling Romance Award and the *RT Book Reviews* Career Achievement Award. Shirley's books have appeared on BlackBoard, *Essence* and *Library Journal* bestseller lists. She is a past president of Romance Writers of America.

Visit the Author Profile page
at Harlequin.com for more titles

To my sister Marilyn, forever in my heart.

CHAPTER ONE

SWEAT TRICKLED DOWN Jason Kendall's neck. It had been years since he'd fled this same road, the wind behind his Corvette creating a small hurricane as he vowed to never set foot on his family's property again. Coming back to Windsor Heights, a town forty miles west of Baltimore, wasn't easy and the closer he got to the farm, the harder it was to hold the memories at bay.

Rain pelted the car windows like large splats of paint falling from the sky. Wiper blades flipped back and forth, clearing the windscreen a second at a time, giving Jace a glimpse of a road that appeared smaller than he remembered. It was a long tree-lined ribbon without lights that led to the house at Kendall Farm. Jace had thought of it as the big house when he lived there. The Kendall, as it was known by the locals, was a world unto itself, but it was a world that was stuck in time. His half brother, Sheldon, made sure of that.

Thinking of Sheldon, Jace almost laughed. Wouldn't he be surprised to find the family's black sheep on his doorstep?

Jason Kendall had grown up here. Maybe grown up was too strong a term for what had happened to him. He supposed he could say it was the place that made him into the man he was today. He was proud, resourceful, cynical and steadfast. Although maturity had curbed his urge to throw a punch as a solution to an argument, he was always ready to stand his ground.

The Kendall was what the farm had been called since the end of the Civil War when Jameson Kendall returned from the conflict to find himself the lone survivor of his family, the others having succumbed to disease or died on the battlefield. It took him five years of hard work to bring it back to a profitable enterprise. As it passed from generation to generation, it had been well maintained but virtually unchanged.

Peering through the rain-soaked window, Jace tried to spot the house. He'd last seen the imposing structure five years earlier, vowing with every fiber of his being that he wouldn't ever return.

But here he was, driving up the narrow road, returning not as the Prodigal son, but still as a son, even if he was illegitimate and merely tolerated. He had a reason for coming back and it outweighed his emotions.

Would the place be the same? Rain obscured his vision, along with the column of trees that lined the driveway. So much had changed in his life in the intervening years. He was more responsible. And he wasn't as angry, yet no one would call him humble.

He hadn't let Sheldon know he was coming. Why should he? Jace frowned. The Kendall was as much his as it was his half brother's, even if their father had referred to Jace in his will as a distant relative. How distant were direct genes? The same blood that flowed through Sheldon's veins flowed through Jace's, "tainted" though it might be.

Jace gripped the steering wheel strongly enough to crush the hard plastic. What would Sheldon say when he saw him? Would he throw him off the property now that he was the sole owner? Jace didn't put it past his brother. The two had never been real brothers, even saying they were friends would be a stretch, but underneath that tough exterior, Jace had the feeling Sheldon wasn't totally indifferent to him. He was simply his father's son.

When the jumbo jet had set down at Dulles Airport, it had been daylight outside. But quickly the light had gone, giving way to the dark, rainy sky. Lightning flashed and in that instant, Jace saw the house. Unconsciously his foot eased off the accelerator and the car rolled to a gentle stop. Windshield wipers tossed water back and forth as Jace stared at the white house that shimmered through the raindrops.

The house grew larger as he approached it. The six-thousand-square-foot structure had sat on five hundred acres for over a century. The other five hundred that comprised the original property boundary was sold during the Depression, but the majority was still intact. Jace remembered times when all six bedrooms had been filled with guests, when the ballroom was bright with music and he couldn't wait to get to the horses in the back stables.

The road ended in a semicircle in front of

the house. For a moment Jace only looked at it. Age didn't show on the old homestead. The pristine white color he remembered was as fresh and new as if the paint job had been completed yesterday. The five-bar fence he'd climb over as a boy was as strong as it had been when he sat atop a horse and raced the wind. The giant lawn, manicured and welcoming even in the darkness, led to the front door.

He let out a relieved breath. Looking over his shoulder, Jace checked on Ari, his four-year-old son sleeping in the backseat. Jace smiled, thinking Ari could sleep through a war. It was because of him that Jace was here. Ari needed a quiet, private place and better medical care than he was getting in South America. So Jace was back on American soil.

He got out of the car. Instead of climbing the front stairs, he stood looking at the house, oblivious of the water drenching him. He could smell freshly cut grass with the faint hint of horseflesh over the rain. He hadn't ridden in years, but he remembered sitting in the saddle and racing across the grounds with Sheldon shouting at him to slow down.

Not that his half brother was concerned about him. He didn't want the horse to suffer a fall.

A smile came easily to Jace. Yet he never thought he'd miss the Kendall. But he had. It wasn't his brother or father that he missed, but the grooms, the horses, the races and the few people he'd become friends with in town. He missed riding, challenging the wind as he edged the horses faster and faster. He missed jumping fences and even the splash of dirty water and flying debris that hit him in the face. He missed the silent rush of exhilaration for that tiny space of time when both he and his steed were airborne. Knowing there would be a reprimand at the end of the ride didn't stop Jace.

Rain smacked his head and shoulders, soaking through his clothes, breaking the memory that held him in place. Quickly, he moved around the car and lifted the still-sleeping Ari onto his shoulder. Taking the wide steps up to the porch, he carried the boy and stopped in front of the century-old door. Jace reached into his pocket and pulled out a key ring he hadn't done more than glance at in ages. He pushed a gold-colored key into the lock. It resisted his effort to turn.

Shifting Ari, Jace tried again, and again the key would not line up with the inside tumblers and release the lock. "Well, it's been five years," he said aloud. He supposed Sheldon had changed the locks in that time. Stepping back, he rang the doorbell. Inside he heard the soft sound of it chiming. Behind him thunder and lightning cut the sky in quick succession.

Peering through the side windows, he noted that other things had changed, too. The runner that led from the door through to the kitchen at the back was gone. A new floor of polished oak gleamed in the semidarkness.

Jace waited several seconds before ringing the bell again. Ari weighed about forty pounds, but he was getting heavy. It was well after midnight and maybe Sheldon and Laura were asleep. If his brother was following their father's method of housekeeping, any help they had would have left hours ago.

Suddenly, a light went on inside the foyer. Jace squinted as the one above his head illuminated at virtually the same moment. Ari squirmed, turning his face toward Jace's neck. Resettling himself, he was asleep without even opening his eyes.

"May I help you?" a voice said through the heavy door.

"You could open the door." Jace peered through the beveled glass trying to see whether it was Laura or someone else.

"Who are you?" she asked. "And what do you want?"

"I'm Jason Kendall and I live here."

There was a long pause before Jace heard the door locks clicking and finally the oval-glass door was pulled open. The light from both the porch and the foyer fell on the woman standing before him. Jace gasped.

"Laura," he whispered, taking a step backward. He thought he was prepared to see her again, but he wasn't.

"I'm not Laura."

Jace stared at her face. He frowned. She wasn't Laura. He blinked several times. This woman only looked slightly like her. Her hair was red with unkempt tendrils that had come loose from the braid that disappeared down her back. Laura, on the other hand, never had a lock of hair out of place.

The young woman appeared weary and tired, wearing exercise pants and a sweat-shirt that came to her knees. "I'm Kelly Ashton. You'd better come out of the rain."

Stepping inside the door was like going back in time. Even though much of what he saw was different, the faint aroma of furniture polish triggered memories he thought were long dead.

Jace brushed passed her and walked several feet into the foyer. The only sounds he heard were his own footsteps as he crossed the floor. The place could have been empty. "Who are you?" he asked as he went into the living room and laid Ari on the sofa. He stood up, taking in the decor of the room. It was completely changed. Laura had probably redecorated. Jace could smell the remnants of a fire that was smoldering in the grate. Even though it was May, the nights in Maryland at this elevation could be nippy. Pulling an afghan that was lying on the back of the sofa over the boy, he turned to examine the woman standing in the doorway.

"Well?" he asked.

"Well what? I told you my name is Kelly Ashton and I live here now."

"You what? Where is Sheldon? Has Laura divorced him? Taken him for all she could get?" Jace could hear the cynicism in his voice. Try as he might, he couldn't remove it when it came to the topic of Laura.

There was silence for a long moment. Then Kelly shook her head.

Jace could see she was a little nervous. He didn't understand why. Who was she? "So, where is my brother?" Jace grimaced. Saying Sheldon's name always left a bad taste in his mouth.

"I think we'd better talk." She stepped back, indicating they should go to another room. Checking Ari one more time, he left his son and followed her.

She went through to the kitchen and pulled open the refrigerator. Without asking, she made him a roast beef sandwich and poured a large glass of orange juice. Jace hadn't realized how hungry he was until she set the food in front of him. Taking a seat at a huge table that hadn't been there five years ago, he took a bite of the sandwich.

"I don't know where your brother is," she began.

"Then why are you living in our house?" Jace asked between mouthfuls.

"It's no longer your house," she said quietly.

"Excuse me?" He stopped eating, nearly choking on the orange juice.

"I own the Kendall. I bought it a couple of years ago."

"What?" he shouted.

"The house was in receivership and I—"

"What's receivership?" he interrupted.

"There were liens against it. Unpaid taxes. Your brother couldn't afford to keep up. He was forced to sell."

"He can't do that." The words burst from Jace.

The woman delivering them sat calmly across from him. She waited a moment, giving him time to calm down.

"I know this is difficult for you to hear. You've been away a long time."

"I'm fine," he said, finishing the sandwich before standing up.

"I was told the property was for sale and I bought it."

"Just like that?"

"Not quite. It took a while to pull my assets together, but I managed."

Jace noticed her eyes were fiery, but her voice remained steady. She was good at holding her emotions in check.

"Where is my brother?" Jace heard the anger in his voice. He and Sheldon had never been on the best of terms, but he had no business selling the house without at least consulting Jace.

"I don't know," she said, and Jace realized he'd asked the question before.

He tried to remember her name. The red hair made him think of Laura. It came to him. *Kelly*.

"There was no reason for him to be involved in the closing. The state had already taken the house and grounds. I don't know where he went once the sale was complete. I heard rumors that he moved out of the state."

Jace hung his head. The pressure of the past few days suddenly came down on him. He and Ari had left Colombia in the midst of political and social turmoil. Ari had asthma and Jace's jobs were often in places that aggravated his condition. He'd watched the child struggling to breathe and knew the child needed better medical care. But the other reason for them to leave Tumaco was the drug war that had broken out nearby. For their own protection, it was time to go. Jace made the decision in a rush of packing, discarding furniture and settling his job. Soon he and Ari had boarded a plane and flown to Mexico. Then on to Washington, DC, where he rented a car and ended their journey at the Kendall. Jace had assumed he could bring the boy home despite his brother's treatment of Jace. He assumed he and his son would have a place to stay.

What would happen to them now? Ari had already lost his mother. He was too young to remember her or her sacrifice to save him. Jace formally adopted the boy, going through a well-run program that advocated for children. He was the only parent Ari had ever known.

Jace thought of his own mother. It had been a long while since he remembered her. She made sacrifices for him, loved him unconditionally, the way he'd come to love Ari. Losing her was painful. It took years of grieving before he could think of her without tears.

He couldn't go to the home they'd had before he came to live at the Kendall. There was nothing there. They'd lived in an apartment in Albany, New York. When his father came to get him, he'd thrown out everything in the apartment. All Jace saved were a few pictures and the jewelry the hospital returned to him. In this he and Ari were nearly the same. Jace had a photo of Ari's mother that he'd taken from the apartment where she had lived.

Ari had no memory of his mother and Jace didn't know if knowing or not knowing was better. He supposed time would tell.

Jace didn't have that much money. Most of it had been spent getting him and Ari to the States. He'd counted on everything at the Kendall being the same. It couldn't be true, he told himself. Sheldon couldn't have sold the house without telling him. Even with the way things were left between them, Jace should have been told. Maybe he could have helped. He couldn't, but Sheldon didn't know that and he never asked.

"What about Laura? Do you know anything about her?" Jace changed the subject.

Jace assumed Kelly's hesitation meant that she knew the history behind Laura and himself. At least she knew the rumors.

"I'm s-sorry to be the one to tell you this," Kelly stuttered. "But I'm afraid she died two years ago."

Jace was stunned. Numbness took over his body. He needed someplace to go. Pacing in the spacious kitchen didn't seem far enough away from the news. He didn't think of Laura often, but he never imagined her dead. Before deciding to come home, Jace had basically folded up the memories of his former time at the Kendall and placed them in a safe corner of his mind, never to be revisited. But life wouldn't let him keep that promise to himself. The memories had been opened as he watched Ari limp across the floor of their tiny apartment in Colombia. Ari loved to climb. Two weeks ago he was running through some trees when he tripped and twisted his foot. The limp was better than it had been. In another few weeks hopefully it would be gone. He looked thin and pale. Jace made the decision to return to Maryland once the shootings started in their neighborhood, and in so doing, to bring Laura and his brother back into his life.

Laura had been perfect for Jace, or so he thought. And that should have been his first clue that life was never going to end with happily-ever-after. But Jason Kendall was too blinded by Laura's beauty to see that their relationship was already skidding.

It was a wonderful wedding. The bride

wore white and had the appropriate amount of mist in her eyes. The groom beamed and the best man—well the best man sat in the audience, witnessing the nuptials between his brother and his former fiancée, feeling like every eye in the huge church wasn't on the bride and groom, but trained with pity on him.

Tucking his hands behind his back, Jace stared at the darkness outside the windows. It was like looking through a time portal, viewing the day he'd met Laura Whitmore and how that had altered the course of his future.

He closed his eyes, failing to block it out.

"Hullo," she had said. It was the first word she'd uttered and it had that deep, sexy sound of a 1930s screen star. He was Jason then. He wouldn't be called Jace for several years. Twenty years old, as green as they come, and just out of college, Jace was ready to conquer the world. Laura looked as if she'd recently stepped off the pages of a fashion magazine—tall, willowy, with dark red hair that shadowed one side of her face and dipped over her shoulder playing hide and seek with one of her breasts.

Jason had been peering at the sky as he

headed for the concession stand. The Firebirds had just flown overhead and most of the patrons of the fall air show were watching their aerial exercises. Unaware that he was close to someone, Jason and Laura collided. Instinctively, his hands came out to steady her. He felt her curves and the softness of her waist. No woman had ever claimed his attention as instantly as she had. He could feel his breath catch and electricity snake through his fingers and up his arms.

"Hello." He only managed to get the one word out, because his eyes were too busy taking in a face more lovely than any he'd seen before. Her eyes were on him, too. Admiring. He shifted his position and glanced away, not wanting her to read the thoughts that were dominant in his head. He probably apologized for walking into her, but no memory of the exchange came to him.

Jason introduced himself then and took the hand Laura offered. And that's where it had begun.

"Have you ever wanted to fly one of those?" she asked later as they'd strolled about the grounds, inspecting the planes on the airfield. She sipped from a bottle of water that hung from a strap over her shoulder.

"What guy hasn't?" Jason answered. "To control all that power and have the freedom of the sky, it's a dream come true."

Dream come true. Today Jace sneered at the irony of the phrase. He thought Laura was the beginning and end of everything he'd searched for in life. From then on, even though she lived in the District of Columbia, and had worked as a researcher for the Air Force for the past two years and he lived in Maryland, a few hours from her, he pursued her.

For them, everything seemed to fit. Neither could see beyond the other, at least he thought that was true for both of them, until that night six weeks after they met, when he brought her home to introduce her to his family. Little did he know that a simple dinner with them would be another turning point in his life. That the fabric of a relationship Jason would have sworn couldn't be ripped, was shredded.

That was the night Laura met Sheldon.

Looking back on it, Jace should have realized. His fire with her had flashed fast and burned bright, but it couldn't match the inferno that surrounded her and his older sibling.

Jason stayed around until their wedding, most of it he couldn't remember the next day or any day since. They left for their honeymoon and he left for parts unknown. He still wasn't sure to this day where he went or what happened to him. Six months later he emerged from a bottle of vodka on the seedy side of some town near Athens in Greece. With no money, no friends and only the sour taste of stale liquor in his mouth, he headed out to find work.

He looked like a homeless drunk. He *was* a homeless drunk. His clothes were dirty and torn and he had difficulty speaking the language. Eventually, Jason found a church, a place where he got a meal. His stomach had growled all day and as soon as he entered the dimly lit shelter and smelled the coffee, he thought he'd gone to heaven.

He speculated how long it had been since he'd eaten. If he ate anything, would it stay down? Sitting at a plain wooden table he ate a little rice and lamb and had another cup of the heavy mud-like coffee.

Jason kept his head down, speaking to no one and likewise no one spoke to him. The coffee was a bottomless cup and it seemed his thirst was unquenchable. He drank so much of the stuff that he thought it would have cured him for a lifetime of ever drinking the liquid again. But later, he discovered an acquired taste for it.

That night he slept in an alley and in the morning, nudged by a not-so-friendly constable, continued his search for a job. He washed up in the sea and, turning his only shirt inside out, did the best he could to look presentable. He got hired washing dishes for half the usual rate, but he couldn't be picky. Meals came with his wages. It wasn't much, but enough to pay for a room for the night and a hot shower. After a week, Jace signed on to a freighter. He didn't care where it was going, east or west didn't matter. Eventually he would get back to the States. What he hadn't expected was to end up fighting for his life in the middle of a South American drug war. But that's where he found Ari. And for the child's sake he would do it all again.

But there was one thing he would never do again. No woman would ever make him feel the way Laura had. She was dead and so was anything that surrounded his feelings for her or any other woman.

"When did she die?" he asked, coming out of the years that bound his old life to this one.

"She died just before your brother lost the house."

Kelly's voice was soft and kind. He wasn't sure he deserved her consideration given how he'd landed here with Ari.

"I'm sorry," she said.

"When I left she was so active, so alive."

"You might talk to some of her friends. I didn't know them."

Jace walked to the window. He looked out on the darkness. "I didn't expect this," he said, more to himself than to Kelly. "I'm not sure what we do now." He turned back to her. "Do you mind if I just rest awhile before making any decisions?"

CHAPTER TWO

A THOUSAND THINGS went through Kelly's mind as she watched Jason Kendall staring through the window. She'd seen all the signs before. He was carrying a torch for his brother's wife. Kelly had lived in Windsor Heights all her life, except for the five years she'd spent in New York after college. She'd heard conflicting versions of the story about Jason Kendall and his brother's wife. You couldn't live in Windsor Heights and not be fascinated by the people living at the Kendall, especially when they were acting less than perfect. And with Jason that was the norm.

Kelly had seen Jason at infrequent times. He always seemed to be away. Kelly doubted he would recognize her.

"What about the child?" she asked. The boy he'd carried in was small and dark, with no resemblance to Jace that she could see in the few seconds she'd glanced at his sleeping figure. "What's his name?"

"Ari. Short for Aristotle."

"Greek," she smiled. "How long have you two been traveling?"

"A couple of days," Jace said. "And he's not Greek."

She stood up. She admitted she shouldn't do this, but she was going to. If Jace had been alone, she'd send him to the nearest hotel, but she couldn't have him waking up a child and taking him out in the rain. And she did know him. If knowing his reputation and living within spitting distance of his home counted for anything, then she did know him. Almost.

"I can offer you a bed for the night. Tomorrow you'll need to make other arrangements."

He didn't say anything, only stared at her.

Kelly couldn't figure out what he was thinking. She felt a little strange. This had been his house before it was hers, but it *was* hers now. And none of the Kendalls had any claim on it.

Maybe Jace wanted to leave right now. Though he obviously didn't know where his brother was, maybe he had friends in Windsor Heights he could go to. The hour was late, and from what she'd discerned no one knew he was coming back tonight.

"Thank you," he finally said. "We'd appreciate that."

Kelly moved when he spoke. Starting for the living room, she glanced over her shoulder to see him following her.

"If you have pajamas for him, you should get them. I'll take him to one of the guest rooms." She stopped, realizing Jason didn't know where the guest rooms were. When he lived here they might not have been guest rooms.

"I'll find you," he said, understanding her thoughts.

Kelly stopped at the door to the living room and watched as Jace continued to the foyer. She went inside and kneeled in front of the boy. He was still asleep, his body curled into a fetal position. She watched him, trying to determine if there was any resemblance to the man she'd just spent time with in her kitchen. Although Ari was a beautiful child, again she found no features common to him and Jason Kendall. Lifting the child and the afghan Jason had covered him with, she found him lighter in weight than she thought he should be, but still heavy for her. She tried to put him on her shoulder, how Jace had held him, but he slipped down her body and she nearly sat him back on the sofa.

"Here, let me," Jace said, coming to her rescue. In two strides he was by her side and taking the small bundle from her arms. He had set a small suitcase on the floor. It took a moment for them to exchange arms and legs. Kelly smelled the rain on Jace. The need to lean in closer and inhale deeply caught her off guard. Quickly, she lifted the suitcase, giving herself something to do to ward off the possibility that she might let her mind go where it wanted to. She turned and led them up the stairs, walking faster than usual.

She hadn't thought about Jace in a while. All her energy was used up renovating the house and grounds. There were nights when she'd walk about the property and remember seeing him recklessly riding a horse over the jumping course. The old horse-racing track was farther away from the main house. Kelly thought Jace used it to annoy his brother.

He'd changed a lot. When she opened the door she would not have known him if he hadn't given his name. The boyish good looks had been replaced with a rugged worldliness and an unhappiness that seemed to ooze from his pores. His body was solid, however. She'd felt that when he'd taken Ari from her grasp. His skin was tanned so he must have been outside a lot. The one thing he still had was the intensity that she had recognized as a teenager when she hung on the back fence and watched him ride.

Reaching the smallest guest room, Kelly switched on the light as she went inside. Rushing to the bed, she pulled the covers back and Jason laid the boy on the sheets. As Jason reached for the suitcase, she stepped out of his way and then left the two of them alone.

He came out of the room several minutes later. Kelly had checked the adjoining room to make sure it was clean and there were towels in the bathroom.

"You can sleep in this room," she directed him.

"That's all right. I'll sleep here with Ari."

"The two rooms are connected through the bathroom," she told him. "It's more comfortable in there. If Ari wakes up and calls for you, you'll be close by. I'm sure, after such a long time traveling, you want someplace comfortable to sleep."

"As tired as I am, I could sleep standing up," he said in a road-weary voice.

"That won't be necessary," she told him with a smile. "Good night."

Kelly left him. She turned to go back downstairs. It was late and she needed to turn off the lights and go to bed herself.

"Kelly," Jason called.

She paused and turned.

"Thank you," he finally said.

Kelly didn't want to look at him. Her emotions were involved. Though clearly, to find out that he'd lost both his home and the woman he once loved in the same day was pushing him to the limit. It was a lot for anyone to handle.

"Good night," was all Kelly could think to say. "It's only one night," Kelly whispered to herself. She owned the house now and no matter what stories she'd heard about Jason Kendall and how his father and brother had treated him, it was only *one* night.

SUNSHINE BLAZED THROUGH the huge windows that looked out on the back lawn.

Kelly opened her eyes and squinted at the brightness. After all the rain the night before, the light seemed especially brilliant. She loved waking to sunshine and always left the drapes open. But it wasn't the light that woke her today. The feeling of being watched encroached upon her sleep.

She was startled to see Ari's eyes, barely higher than the coverlet, peering at her.

"Am I dead?" he asked.

Kelly blinked, pushing herself up on her elbows to see his entire face.

"Ari, why would you think you're dead?"

"Everything is so white. And you're an angel. Only an angel would know my name," he answered in childlike logic.

Kelly looked at her bedroom. The cover was white, the rug was white and the walls were white. The totally white room had splashes of color in the throw pillows, and gold accents that Kelly had used to decorate the space. "Well, thank you," she said. "But I am not an angel."

"This is what the priest said heaven was like, except…" He trailed off.

"Except what?" Kelly prompted.

"Except for your wings." He tried to look

behind her as if she was hiding her angel wings within the folds of the bed cover.

Kelly laughed. "You're not dead, Ari."

He frowned and looked around the room, up at the ceiling, at her bed, and then back at her. "This isn't heaven?"

"This is my bedroom."

"All by yourself?" His eyes opened wide.

"I'm afraid so."

"Wow!" he said. "Is my room for only me?" He pointed to himself as his boy-soprano voice went up hopefully at the end of the sentence.

Kelly sat fully up. She couldn't tell the child he wouldn't be staying. She'd only given Jason Kendall and his son a room for the night. Today they had to go.

"Where's your father?" she asked instead of answering his question.

"I don't know. Is he dead, too?"

"Ari, you're not dead and neither is your dad."

"What is this place? My dad said we were coming to his old house. This doesn't look like a old house."

Kelly stopped herself from correcting the

boy's grammar. "Actually, this is a very old house. It was built a long time ago."

"Before I was born?"

Kelly smiled. "Before your father was born," she told him. "People will want to come and see it when it's complete. A lot of work has been done to make it look like it did back then."

"Did you do it?"

She smiled. She'd forgotten that kids ask a lot of questions. "Yes, Ari, I did a lot of it." Pushing her arms into the robe that matched her nightgown, she asked, "Are you hungry?"

He quickly began bobbing his head up and down.

"Good, then you can't be dead. Because dead people don't get hungry."

He seemed to be weighing the truthfulness of that in his four-year-old mind. After a moment he nodded and she guessed he agreed with her.

"How about we go and get something to eat?" Kelly didn't wait for an answer. She offered her hand and he took it. The two went downstairs to the kitchen.

"Wow," he said again as they entered the

spacious kitchen. "I never saw a room this big."

Kelly was getting a picture of how they must have lived. Their home was probably a lot smaller in comparison. The house at the Kendall, constructed in 1860 by Caldwell Kendall on land that was a bequest upon his marrying a nearby landowner's daughter, couldn't be called a farmhouse. It wasn't a purely serviceable structure. The Kendall was built to display the grandeur of the time.

The place had been magnificent when Kelly was a little girl. What it looked like when she bought it was another story. Slowly she was trying to give it back that glory. But it was expensive and she was having to find alternative means to keep it solvent.

"Do you like waffles?" she asked.

"What's waffles?"

It was her turn to be surprised. "You've never had a waffle? Well, today is your lucky day."

Kelly was used to fending for herself. She hadn't grown up in the shadow of the luxury that was the Kendall. Her home was a small house a few miles away. Losing her mother when she was ten, she was raised by her father. He'd worked as a groom at a nearby farm, making barely enough money to make ends meet. Most of his money he drank before getting home. When he did come home, she'd take whatever she could find to buy food. Consequently, Kelly learned to make meals from practically nothing. And she never wasted anything.

She had a maternal grandmother living in Arizona and several cousins she'd heard of, but never seen. After her own mother died, she was too young to think of going to live with her grandmother and her father hadn't begun to drink yet. By the time Kelly was old enough to think of leaving, she felt her father needed her. They'd fallen into a routine. While she couldn't keep him from drinking, there was a weird stability to their relationship.

The Kendall had a part-time cook and housekeeper. The housekeeper came once a week and did the heavy cleaning. It was Kelly's plan to increase her hours when the Kendall was self-sustaining.

"Can I pour now?" Ari asked after she'd stirred the mix.

"Ari, you speak English really well, how did that happen?"

"My dad taught me."

Kelly smiled. Close enough, she thought.

While it had taken Kelly nearly six months to repair and replace the kitchen, she could say it was now properly christened. A fine coat of flour blanketed the surface of the granite counter and part of the floor. The waffle iron had burned sap oozing over the sides. And Kelly's white angelic nightgown and robe were stained down the front with grape juice. Ari didn't fair well, either. The grape stains on his pajamas trailed from neck to toe and his bronze-colored hands were white with flour.

"It's my turn to pour," Ari insisted.

"You bet it is," Kelly told him. "But you have to be careful because this is very hot." She pointed to the waffle iron.

"I can do it," he assured her.

"All right. Are you ready?"

"Ready," he said with a big smile on his face.

Kelly handed him a small mixing bowl with just enough batter to fill the waffle iron.

"Evenly," she whispered. He made wide

circles with the bowl, spreading the batter over the iron and watching it melt together to cover the surface.

"Now close the top," she instructed.

He handed her the bowl and the two of them lowered the hot lid.

"Good," she said. While they waited, Kelly finished the bacon and eggs and poured herself a cup of coffee. She hazarded to give Ari another cup of grape juice, only this time she found a cup and fashioned a top. Ari opened the waffle iron and, while the shape of the iron was circular, she flipped the strangely shaped trapezoid onto a plate. At the table seconds later, Ari dug into his breakfast. With his mouth full, he said, "I like it. Can we have these every day?"

There was that permanent question again. Ari thought he was here for good. Jason had told him they were coming here, coming home. Only he didn't know about the sale. This wasn't their home and Kelly couldn't take them in. She was having a hard enough time getting the place back on its feet.

Ari took another bite of the syrupy confection. "I like it," he said again. He put another forkful of food in his mouth then stopped and lowered his fork. He put his hands in his lap, looking down as if he shouldn't be enjoying his meal.

"Is something wrong?" Kelly asked.

"Is my dad going to eat with us?"

"I'm sure he's still asleep," Kelly said. Jason had been dead on his feet last night and it was well past one o'clock when she'd shown him the room where he could sleep.

"He always eats breakfast with me," Ari said.

"We could wake him up, but he's very tired," Kelly told him. "Do you think you can eat with me? Just this once?"

He cocked his head in a questioning manner and considered her offer. "He's been tired before, but he always ate with me."

"How about this," Kelly asked. "When he wakes up, you can eat with him again?"

Ari smiled. Apparently, she'd hit upon the perfect solution. "I guess that's all right." Picking up his fork, he resumed his meal.

Kelly figured it would be lunchtime before Jason opened his eyes. She'd let him sleep. Ari was a delightful child. He had dark curly hair and eyes that were practically black. He was thin and limped slightly when he walked.

Without a resemblance to Jace, Kelly thought Ari must look like his mother.

She wondered where his mother was now. Suddenly a terrible thought occurred to her. Suppose Jason had kidnapped his son and brought him here without the mother's consent? After all, he'd shown up in the middle of the night without a place to stay and with a child. This could be trouble, she thought. And she'd had enough of that to last a lifetime.

THAT WAS THE best dream Jace had ever had. He and Ari played on a hill. They were safe. He knew nothing would happen to them there. Father and son ran, jumped and rolled over the ground. Jace heard his son laughing. He didn't wheeze or limp, but hung on tightly when Jace swung him around in circles. Waking, he held on to the image for a moment longer.

Opening his eyes was a shock.

He didn't know where he was. Sitting up in bed, his thoughts rushed to Ari. Where was he? Then it came back to him. Jace remembered.

He was home.

Pushing the covers aside, he went to the

bathroom's connecting door and into the room where Ari slept. The boy was gone. The bed had been made and other than the suitcase sitting open on a bench at the end of the bed, there was no sign that his son had ever been in this room.

Jace didn't think about his appearance until he was halfway to the door. He turned around and ran back to the guest room. This wasn't his room. When he lived here, this had been a guest room, but it didn't connect to the room next door and neither of them had been decorated as they were now. Where he'd slept, the walls were a light blue. The bedding on the four-poster was mainly white, but picked up the same blue wall color in subtle stripes. Jace remembered it with gray walls and heavy furniture.

Ari's room was a light green with white molding. His bedding was yellow and the boy required a step stool to reach the mattress. Formerly, the walls had been white and the bed smaller than the queen-size that sat there now.

Pushing his legs into his pants, Jace glanced out the window and stopped. Ari was outside.

With Kelly.

They were playing with a ball. He was teaching her soccer moves. Jace stared as his son bounced the ball off his knees and feet. Then he offered the ball to Kelly and she tried to imitate his moves. Jace laughed. It was hilarious to watch her. She showed no signs of embarrassment by being shown up by a four-year-old. Her hair bounced in the morning light. Copper highlights flickered, changing color with every movement of her head. When the ball fell to the ground and Kelly missed it, she ran after it. Ari limped after her. She tripped and fell. Ari went down with her. They both laughed. Jace laughed, too.

They looked good together. Ari had asthma, but he wasn't coughing or wheezing and he didn't look as if his breath was labored. Jace felt relief. This confirmed it was the correct decision to bring the boy here. Although now that they didn't have a place to stay and Jace had no job, their lives were in flux. Jace had to stay strong for them both; he'd figure something out.

First he had to find them a place to stay. This was no longer the Kendall Farm he had known. Coming back here, specifically, had been a mistake. Jace had hoped things would change.

And they had.

But not in his favor.

CHAPTER THREE

"DAD," ARI SHOUTED and took off running across the back porch. He threw open the screen door and launched himself into the kitchen. Even though he favored his left leg, Jace caught him as he propelled himself into his arms. The momentum of the ball of energy turned Jace completely around. "We waited a long time," Ari said. "You were asleep. Kelly said you were tired." He glanced at her, wobbling precariously in Jace's arms. "We let you sleep. But we already ate. Two times." He put up two fingers, running on with his explanation of their day.

"That's all right, sport." Jace kissed the boy on the top of his head. He looked at Kelly, who'd come into the kitchen behind Ari. "Thank you," he said. "I didn't intend to sleep the day away."

She smiled. Jace thought she looked familiar when he saw that smile and tried to recall if he'd ever seen her before.

"We were outside playing," Ari informed him. "I showed Kelly how to play soccer. She's not very good." He frowned, shaking his head, his expression very serious. "She needs to practice." He pronounced the words very precisely.

Kelly laughed, raising her hand to cover her mouth. Something about the gesture grabbed Jace's attention. A tiny trickle of awareness seeped inside him.

"Good morning." He openly admired her. She was dressed in a short-sleeved T-shirt that stopped at her waist. It was met by a pair of light blue shorts that showed off her long legs. Jace found his eyes traveling the distance from the running shoes on her feet to the hair she'd let fall behind her shoulders.

"It's not morning, Dad," Ari said and tugged on his arm. Jace realized his son had repeated the sentence.

"I know," he commented and with a kiss to his forehead set him on his feet.

Kelly opened the refrigerator and pulled out two drink bottles of orange juice. "Can you drink from the bottle?" she asked Ari.

"Yes," he said reaching for it.

She loosened the top. Jace heard the snap as the seal was broken. She handed it to Ari.

"Why don't you go and drink that on the porch?" Jace suggested.

Ari moved out the back door and Jace waited until his son was seated on the porch steps before addressing Kelly. She, too, was watching Ari. He didn't know how to begin to say what he needed to say.

"He's a wonderful child," she said.

"I'm very proud of him." He could tell she had questions about Ari. It was obvious by Ari's black eyes and curly dark hair that none of Jace's features were present in him. "Go ahead, ask."

"Ask what?"

"Ask about Ari's adoption," he said.

"He's adopted?"

Jace saw her shoulders drop as if she were relieved. "Does that make a difference?" He raised his eyebrows skeptically.

She came up in front of the counter that separated them. "I'm ashamed to admit what I was thinking."

"And what was that?" Jace braced himself

for some prejudicial comment. He'd seen people react to the two of them before.

"You don't recognize me, do you?"

"What?" He didn't follow her thought patterns.

She shook her head quickly. "Of course, you wouldn't. I used to live a couple of miles from here."

"You did?" Was that why he felt he'd seen her before?

"In Short Hills," she told him.

Suddenly, it dawned on him what and where Short Hill was. It was a poor area, run-down, with low-income housing and a lot of crime, a place where people double- and triple-locked doors that a good puff of wind could blow down. Anyone with an address there was immediately judged as a drunk or criminal. Jace now understood her logic. She wasn't judging Ari's paternity.

"I used to come by here on my way home from school," Kelly said. "I saw you a few times, but of course, your reputation was known even in Short Hills."

He swallowed, remembering the rebellious young man he'd once been. He had good reason, but there was no need to burden her with it. "I'm no longer that person."

"I understand. I'm a different person from the little girl who used to live in Short Hills. When I left there, I moved to New York. If Short Hills didn't teach me self-protection, the city did.

"I thought you'd kidnapped Ari and fled Colombia. And that I was now harboring a fugitive."

Jace stared at her for a long moment. Then a bubble of laughter pushed into this throat and he smiled. Unable to stop it, the laughter poured from him. She smiled a little in response, but didn't join him in the merriment that gripped him. He didn't tell her what he'd been thinking.

"I suppose, from your point of view, it might look like that." He could hardly get the sentence out. It was absurd that he'd kidnapped Ari. Ari came into his life due to crazy circumstances and there was nothing else he could do short of abandoning the child.

Adopting a child wasn't ever his first instinct, though now that he had Ari, he hated being apart from him, even for a moment.

"Well, what was it like then?"

She was a hard cookie, Jace thought. Sure she had grown up in a rough area, but he bet he could match her experience for experience. Jace shook his head.

"I have all our important papers in the car. I'll get them if you want to see them."

He turned to go.

"That won't be necessary," she said, halting him in his tracks. "Does he know?" She glanced at Ari, still sitting outside.

"He knows. He doesn't remember his parents. His father abandoned them when Ari was born. His mother worked in a cocaine factory."

Kelly gasped.

Jace watched her. "I didn't know her, didn't know there was a cocaine factory until later. I'd seen her once or twice, but we'd never spoken."

Just as she'd done last night, she opened the refrigerator and pulled out the makings of a meal.

"Would you like breakfast or lunch?" she asked.

"You don't have to cook for me."

"I know," she said. "But you've traveled for two days and slept for the better part of another, I assume you're hungry."

"Isn't there a cook, a housekeeper? When my father was alive, there was a full staff to take care of the place."

"Things have changed," she said flatly. "Now, breakfast or lunch?"

"I think we need to talk," he said.

"Lunch," she answered.

Unlike last night, when she'd made him a sandwich, today she pulled a tray out of the refrigerator and popped it into the oven. Then she forked spaghetti onto a plate, added sauce and placed it in the microwave.

"Ari, time to wash your hands." She called him from the screen door. Her voice was soft and sweet and again Jace thought there was something familiar about her. He chalked it up to the red hair and pushed the thought aside.

Opening the oven door, she pulled out the tray, which he could see now contained garlic bread. The bell rang on the microwave signaling it had completed its flash-heating of food. Soon the three of them were seated at the table with piping hot garlic bread, salads and steaming plates of pasta.

Ari ate hungrily, shoveling food into his mouth as if he hadn't eaten in days.

"Slow down, Ari," Jace cautioned.

"This is really good," he said, swallowing an amount that was too large for his mouth. "It's nothing like yours."

Kelly laughed. "I guess we both get insulted today."

"Can I say that?" Ari looked at Jace.

"Say what?"

"Insulted? Is it a bad word?"

"It's not a bad word, but you need to know when to use it," Jace explained. "So for now, don't say it."

With a nod, he went back to his meal. Jace looked up at Kelly. Her gaze was soft as she stared at him. Jace had seen those eyes before. He glanced down at his food. What he had to tell her was hard enough. With her looking at him like that, it was too much.

"Dad, this isn't a hotel, is it?" Ari's mind jumped like lightning from subject to subject. "It doesn't look like the other hotel."

"This isn't a hotel, Ari."

"Our apartment at home wasn't this old."

"No. It wasn't. This house is very old, constructed so long ago, even I wasn't around when it was built."

Ari continued eating. Kelly liked their banter, but she didn't join in the conversation.

Ari finished eating and quickly stood up. "May I go?" he asked. "I want to play some more."

Jace looked at Kelly. She nodded.

"Stay close to the house," he said. "This is a big farm. I don't want you getting lost."

"I won't," he said and rushed out the door and down the back steps. Jace could see he was happy here. He was still in the explorer mode. Everything was new, different and exciting for him. He hadn't had time to get homesick yet.

"I apologize," Kelly said.

"For what?" Jace brought his attention back to her.

"For my thoughts. Obviously, you and Ari have a special relationship. And he's not a kidnapped child."

"Apology accepted."

"Now, you wanted to talk about something," she said. She crossed her arms on the end of the table and gave him her full attention. "Talk."

"I want my home back."

KELLY HAD DEALT with difficult clients before. She'd worked for a marketing firm in New York City and everyone at the firm thought they were more important than anyone else. Among other things, she'd learned to steel her features. She remained where she was, refusing to show how upset she was over Jace's statement. His eyes were clear and there was no joke in his comment. He was serious.

"I'm afraid that is not an option," she said calmly. "The house was sold and the deed duly recorded. You can check the county records if you wish. The courthouse is—" She didn't get any further.

"I know where the courthouse is," he snapped.

"Don't speak to me like that, Jason." She intentionally used his given name, hoping it brought her point home. "I bought this property free and clear. Your brother had run it into the ground, selling off anything and everything he could. He hadn't paid the taxes in more years than your son is old. I came along and saved it. And I am spending everything I can beg, borrow or steal to make it a going operation. So don't come in here and tell me you're planning to force me out. It isn't going to happen." She took a breath. "I offered you one night's lodging. Well, you've had it. You can pack your things and move on. You are no longer welcome here."

Kelly stood up and took her coffee cup to the sink.

"Kelly. You misunderstood me."

She turned around. Jace was now standing within feet of where she was.

"Your words seemed pretty clear to me." Kelly understood that he was back-peddling. What did he expect her reaction to be? Should she just curl up and let him take away everything she'd done in the past two years? She was preparing to open the house to the public and take income from the tours. Sometime in the future, she'd bring back the horses and build a racetrack. Every penny she had was invested in this farm. She had to succeed. Failure was not an option. Not this time.

"I'd like to keep an eye on Ari. Would you mind if we took a walk outside?"

"Okay."

Falling in step, they began to walk, going to the back porch and watching Ari as he played hide and seek with the open barn door.

"Is he all right over there?" Jace asked.

Kelly heard the fatherly concern in his voice. She thought of her own father. With all his faults, he loved his daughter.

"We've already renovated the barn."

"We?"

"My cousin and her husband and I do most of the work. It's hard and we're slow, but it saves us a lot of labor costs."

"You and two other people are working the Kendall?"

She spread her hands. "We're all there is." The barn had been in particularly bad condition when Kelly had taken over the property. An engineering study told her it was structurally sound. The house was livable, although it needed a lot of upgrading. Kelly moved in and asked her cousin and her husband to help her out with the renovations. Drew, her cousin's husband, owned a construction company and she was indebted to him for life.

"Tell me how you came to buy the Kendall?" he asked.

"The cousin who helps me, Mira, and her

husband, Drew, let me know about the property before the for sale sign went up. He knew I always loved it. I immediately called and arranged to tour the place." She glanced at Jace. Jace had his gaze on his son. "It didn't matter what state it was in. I was determined to make it mine."

"Why?"

Kelly surveyed the area. The May weather had turned the grass emerald green. She remembered when it was high enough to hide her five-foot-five frame and coarse enough to leave cuts and bruises on her arms and legs. Now she could look clear across the vista.

"I grew up not far from here."

"Short Hills, you said."

"When I was still in school I used to get off the school bus and climb onto the fence just to watch the horses."

Jace snapped his fingers. "The redhead," he said. "I saw you there a few times. You were only a child."

She was older than she looked, but she didn't say that.

"You weren't here often," she said.

He frowned, but waited for her to continue.

"I know your dad sent you to boarding

school. I thought it must be a wonderful place to go to school, but I didn't see how you could bear to leave the Kendall."

"It wasn't my choice," he admitted.

Kelly knew that. Gossip spread easily around Windsor Heights then and now. Some she'd met since buying the Kendall had told her stories of the Kendall family. It wasn't always pleasant.

"You haven't told me why you love it here," Jace said.

Her throat closed and she had to swallow the emotion that rose in her. "I've always felt I was part of this land. And that this is where I was supposed to be. When I bought it, it needed a lot of work. And I mean a lot. But I loved doing it. I loved seeing it come back to the glory it once had. I want to make it into a showplace. And every floor I restore, every nail I use to repair something is part of me going into the history of this place."

"But you're not a Kendall."

The words hurt for some reason. She would never be a Kendall. "That's true, but...I belong here. I feel it. I suppose it was because I grew up so close to the place. The Kendall had survived war and depression, and I wanted to be a survivor, too, in my own way." Things were often out of sorts in her own home. The Kendall was her anchor.

"Why haven't you changed its name then? You've been here two years."

She shook her head, still smiling. "It wouldn't be the same. For over a century this has been the Kendall. Changing a name would change the nature of the place."

"Do you know where my brother is?" He abruptly switched subjects.

"I haven't seen him. In fact, I never saw him. The entire transaction was completed between the bank and the county. Your brother wasn't ever required to be there."

"Why didn't he pay the taxes? Sheldon loved being the lord of the manor."

"I don't know. People in town said it was mismanagement. Given the state of the property when I showed up, it wouldn't be hard to believe."

"It wasn't necessary to the sale," Jace said, and Kelly heard the censure in his voice.

"It wasn't my business," she told him. "I didn't force your brother to get into trouble with his finances and there was no reason why I should help him if that's what you're implying."

"Ari, don't do that," Jace shouted. He was on his feet, ready to run and aid his son if necessary.

Kelly quickly followed Jace's gaze to where the child stood. His foot was in mid-air as if he'd been paralyzed by the urgency in Jace's voice. Ari had been about to climb a ladder propped up on the side of the barn. It wouldn't take much for Ari to tumble over.

"I should think you'd be glad someone who really cares about the Kendall bought it," she said. "It could have gone to a developer who would raze the house and subdivide it into apartments or condos."

She left him then and went into the house. She had work to do and she was grossly behind getting started.

THIS WAS NOT the homecoming Jace expected.

Rushing forward, he headed for Ari. When the boy saw him coming, he took off and ran for him. His weak leg dragged a little behind, but Ari compensated. Already Jace thought he was doing better. He hadn't had a problem with his asthma today; surely Kelly would have told him if Ari had had restricted breathing.

"Dad, can we go in the barn?" he asked, instinctively taking his hand and pulling him in that direction.

"Let's go look at where the horses used to live," Jace said.

"Wow! Horses!"

The barn was a few hundred feet from the house. While the weather last night had been wet, the grass under their feet was already dry. Jace thought the silence was eerie. Back in his day, he should have heard the horses by now.

Jace pulled the barn door open all the way, waiting a moment for his eyes to adjust before stepping into the dim light. Ari scampered forward, eager to see.

The faint scent of horse manure and cleanser permeated the air. Jace frowned as anger stole over him. The horses had been his sanctuary. How dare Sheldon let the Kendall fall apart to the point where there were no horses here.

Their great-great-grandfather had provided for the upkeep of the house by investing in and training horses, race horses especially.

Evidently, he was very good at it since he forged a legacy that had continued for generations. It was Sheldon's legacy and Jace's, too—no matter what his father thought—to keep it alive by offering the best in boarding and rearing horses. And now they were gone.

"Where are the horses, Dad? Are they all in Texas?"

Ari had no concept of the size of the United States. Texas could have been on the other side of the barn as far as he knew. He'd seen horses on television and the logic of a four-year-old jumped to explain.

"I don't know where they are, Ari."

"We'll have to ask Kelly," he said positively. "She will know."

Jace doubted that.

KELLY MASSAGED HER temples as she studied father and son from her office window. They disappeared around the side of the horse barn. She knew Jace loved horses. He'd ride as if the devil himself was after him, but then he'd spend an hour in the barn, making sure to cool down the treasured animal.

Eventually, she wanted to have horses boarding here, and if possible, expand the operation even further. Some day she planned on having allowance races run here, and eventually move up to stakes races. But she had other things to do with the small amount of money she still had in her account.

Telling herself she'd deal with Jace later, she pulled her hair into a long ponytail and went to the library. It was the last unfinished room in the house. It needed to be painted and decorated.

With all the prep work done, it was time to put the paint on the walls. Kelly scrubbed her roller up and down in the pan to prevent drips and raised it to the wall. The soft blue transformed the space. She liked it already. The steady action gave her time to think.

What was she going to do with Jason Kendall and his son? And why did she believe it was her duty to do anything? Jace was a grown man. He had to be nearing thirty by now. He seemed to be responsible, at least where Ari was concerned. She'd given them one night only. He should be searching for a new place to stay, instead of hanging out at an estate he never owned. His own father mustn't have thought much of him to do that to him. That was the rumor Kelly had heard.

She'd felt sorry for Jace at the time. She realized that as a kid she'd been caught up in how things looked around here. That just because the Kendalls had a lovely house and lovely horses, didn't mean their family was any less troubled than hers. It occurred to her that there were some old files and family photos she'd moved into the attic, since the sale of the property had included all of the furnishings.

It was as if Sheldon had walked away with only the clothes on his back. She supposed she should give those items to Jace.

The blue wall looked beautiful. She stepped back, analyzed her work. Smiling, she thought when the books were brought back into the room, it would be a welcome place to sit and read.

Kelly dropped her shoulders. She felt an allegiance to Jace, although that made no sense. She hadn't known him well while they were growing up, but he was a Kendall. And this had been his home once.

Maybe she should give him a job. The place could use his help. He could stay until he found a place of his own.

Stepping back, she said, "Yes, that works."

Though her eyes were on the wall, she was talking about Jace.

"Kelll-ly!"

She heard Ari's sweet voice calling her name.

"Down here," she hollered.

She heard footsteps running toward the room. The door was already open for ventilation. Ari found her and rushed forward.

"Don't run," she told him, lifting a hand to catch him.

Too late. His little body sailed across the drop cloth. His feet came out from under him and he slipped, momentum carrying him several feet before he stopped.

Jace was on his heels behind him. Kelly grabbed the paint tray and held it still. Then she faced Jace.

"Are you all right?" she asked the child.

Ari looked up. "That was fun. Can I do it again?"

Jace let out the breath he must have been holding. "No, you cannot," he said.

Kelly, who was on her knees, sat back on her legs. "Are you sure you're okay?"

Ari nodded.

Jace looked at the walls and immediately

took in the one Kelly had been working on. "Did he do any damage?"

"I don't think so. But he might have a bruise tomorrow on his legs. There's hardwood under this tarp."

Jace examined Ari, pulling his pant leg aside and looking at him.

"Dad," Ari protested and pulled his clothes back. "Not in front of her." His voice was a stage whisper.

Kelly turned her head. "I won't look. I promise."

"I think you'll live," Jace said several seconds later.

"Where are the horses?" Ari asked.

Subject changes were no problem for four-year-olds Kelly was finding.

"We went to the horse barn," Jace explained. "It's empty."

"Well, Ari, the former owner sold the horses in an attempt to pay off the debt on the Kendall."

Jace's jaw clenched. She understood his frustration. Since arriving here, everything he thought he knew was gone, starting with Laura. And although Kelly had nothing to do with any of it, she could see that this proud man was hurting.

"What are we gonna do now, Dad?" Ari, unaware of any of the adults' feelings, was ready for the next adventure.

"Ari, would you like to see some pictures of horses?" she asked.

"Wow, yeah."

"They're on the table in the big living room down the hall. Do you remember where that is?"

He looked at his dad as if Jace might deny the chance to him. Jace nodded.

"Yes. I remember." Ari started to move, but Jace restrained him.

"Walk," his father said.

The little boy walked out of the room with both adults watching him.

"I have a proposal for you," she told Jace.

"What is it?"

She saw him stiffen. "You're an engineer?"

He nodded.

"What kind of engineer?"

"Civil," he said, his voice almost a challenge.

"Does that mean you know about bridges and roads, things like that?"

"It does. I also know about water lines and—"

"How about construction?" she interrupted.

"Some."

"I'd like to offer you a job."

"What?"

"Do you have one? Someplace to go? I thought your showing up here last night was the last stop on a long journey."

"It was," he said. "What kind of job?"

"As an engineer, of sorts. Although, I can't pay you what an engineer probably makes, I can offer room and board for you and Ari and a small wage. You can consider it temporary until you find something better."

He mulled that over for a moment. "What do I do?"

"You help me get the rest of this property in shape."

He looked around the library. The ceiling and trim work had been done. She was making headway on the walls. The shelves were gleaming white and leaning against a door on the other side of the room.

"It looks like you have everything under control." His gaze swept back to her.

"Don't go by the condition of the house. I have some serious issues that need attention."

"Like what?"

"Irrigation, for one. You said you knew about water. I want to make sure there's proper runoff and drainage for the pastures and build safer pathways around the grounds."

"You expecting a lot of visitors?"

"Yes, hopefully," she said. "What about it? Will you take the job?"

"Dad!" Ari came bounding back, running fast and hard. He stopped just before careening into Jace. "Can I get my own horse?"

Jace turned and looked at Kelly. "Maybe," he said.

CHAPTER FOUR

WINDSOR HEIGHTS WASN'T exactly on the cutting edge of the twenty-first century, though as Jason drove into town he noticed how different the place looked. Because he had often been away for long periods of time with boarding school, college and working, Jace's trips back to the Kendall made him more able to see the changes as sweeping rather than subtle. First, the number of cars on the street alone could cause a traffic jam. As far as he knew, there had never been a traffic jam in Windsor Heights. There were new stores along Main Street. He saw that the old dress shop had had a facelift. The bookstore was gone, replaced by an office supply store. The bank, however, was in the same place and while it was five years older, it appeared as new as it had been when it was built.

Jace opened its heavy door and walked through. Nothing here was different. The loan office was in the same place and Jace went directly toward it.

"Jason! Jason Kendall." Someone called his name. "Is that you? I can't believe it. I haven't seen you in years."

A man behind a glass wall stood up and came out, his hand outstretched. Jace took it, recognizing him only after he was already pumping his hand.

"Kurt Mallard," Jace said, grateful to find someone he'd once known. "Who would have thought?"

"Come on in and sit down a minute. Tell me what brings you back to Windsor Heights?"

Jace noticed his door had Kurt Mallard, Loan Officer printed on it in small black letters.

"My home," he said. Jace took a seat. "I'm here about the Kendall."

Kurt frowned. "It's a shame about that." Then his face cleared and the frown was replaced with a smile.

"But it seems the new owner is working miracles restoring it. Have you met her yet?"

Jace didn't get to answer.

Kurt continued, "She's a beauty. Got flaming red hair. When she's in here and the sun shines through that window..." He pointed to a window outside the office "It's like fire."

"I've met her," Jace cut in.

Kurt chuckled and cleared away some papers on his desk.

"So you're the loan officer," Jace pointed out.

"Never thought I'd make it, did you?"

Kurt had been the other bad boy of Windsor Heights. While the two of them rarely cut up together, Jace knew of him, his antics and the gang he ran around with. None of them were people Jace cared to be associated with. Kurt was on the school's football team and many people looked the other way at the things he did for that reason. Jace was the prep school kid, the rich kid, the one who lived in the big house. He wasn't welcome by even the bullies of the area. After that Jace lost track of Kurt. But now Kurt worked at the bank and Jace's family no longer owned the big house. That privilege was held by a determined redhead unafraid to get her hands dirty.

"Kurt, I'm here for a loan," Jace said, opting for the cold, hard truth.

Kurt shifted in his chair. "Okay," he said. "What's the loan for?"

"I want to buy the Kendall."

Kurt smiled warmly. "This is great. I'm glad Ms. Ashton is willing to sell it back to you. After all, the Kendall should be owned by a Kendall." He laughed a hearty sound.

"Well, there's a slight issue there."

"What's the problem?"

"I only got back into town last night. I have a little money, but I'd need a big mortgage."

Kurt leaned forward. "So far, that seems like something we might be able to work out." He reached sideways and pulled a packet of documents out of a vertical file stand.

"The only collateral I have is my name."

Jace watched him visibly recoil.

"Has Ms. Ashton agreed to allow you to take over the mortgage?"

Jace shook his head.

"Does she even know you're here?"

Again he shook his head.

"I'm afraid I'm not going to be able to help you, Jason. Besides having no collateral and no agreement from the owner to sell, currently you're unemployed, I assume. The bank requires at least that you have a job in order for me to approve a loan. I'm afraid even filling out the paperwork will be of no use." He looked at the packet on his desk.

"I do have a job," Jace said.

"Where?"

"It's at the Kendall."

"You have a job at the Kendall?" The eyebrows went up.

Jace nodded.

"How long have you worked there?"

"I only got back yesterday."

"So you begin tomorrow?" Kurt asked.

"Yes, tomorrow."

"That's not going to be long enough. For a mortgage, which you don't qualify for, we need several pieces of paperwork, including your last three check stubs. I'm sorry Jace."

"I have those. I worked in South America."

"Good. What did you do there?"

"I'm an engineer. I worked on a water pipeline."

"Do you own any property?"

Jace shook his head.

Kurt frowned. "I can give you the paperwork. It will tell you what we require, but without a willingness to sell from Ms. Ashton, it's likely a waste of time."

Jace stood up. "Thanks anyway," he said. Jace knew it would be a problem getting money, but he had to try. His son's well-being was at stake. He shook hands with Kurt and left.

Out on the street, Jace went to his car and got in. He didn't start the engine. He sat thinking, wanting to come up with something he could do to get his house back. Kurt had said he was a Kendall and a Kendall should own the property that had been in his family since the Civil War. With the way he'd been treated, sometimes even he wondered why the house meant so much to him. It shouldn't. But it did.

When he left years ago, angry at the world and everything in it, he wanted nothing but to get as far from the Kendall as he could. But running away didn't take the place out of him. He missed it, missed the horses and the riding. He missed the familiarity of it, even the safety. While his father and brother weren't model parent and sibling, he had enough distractions to ignore their influence on him. And he did what he liked.

Yet when he was in South America he longed for the Kendall. He told himself Ari was the reason for his return and that was the truth, but it wasn't the whole truth. Jace had been stumbling around the world, trying to forget, but it was useless. He missed home, wanted to go back. Ari was only the catalyst he used to make the decision.

And now he was here. And everything was different. He was back, but he wasn't home. He was still the stable boy, trying to win over the new lady of the manor.

SHELDON PULLED THE door of his beach bungalow closed. He was headed to the dock to complete a day's work. He squinted at the bright sunshine. Then he heard the laughter. He knew it was in his mind because it was Laura's laugh, her sound. He thought of the photo of her in a frame next to his bed. Her picture was the only thing he'd kept from the Kendall.

She was gone now. Sheldon wanted to remember her only as she'd been in the photo, smiling, dressed in a beautiful gown and standing on the staircase at the Kendall. Their lives were tangled, twined together like the never-ending root system of the common mangrove tree.

After he and Laura married, Jason took off. Neither he nor Laura spoke of him. It became a silent, wordless rule.

Sheldon always wondered why his father never thought of Jason as a son. Not wanting to risk the old man's wrath, Sheldon hadn't asked for a reason. Laura felt it was a sore point with Sheldon, since initially she had come to the Kendall with Jason, and Sheldon, following his father's lead, had almost nothing to do with him, either. It's as if he didn't exist in their world. But that world had disappeared.

Sheldon went back to work. He bent down and scraped. The barnacles fell off the hull and onto the tarp he'd placed on the wharf. He thought of Laura. She'd been the light of his life. Everything he did and thought revolved around her. He'd been a better man with Laura.

After Laura died, Sheldon had no fight left in him. He couldn't do anything, couldn't concentrate on anything, especially the Kendall. When he came out of his grief enough to notice the farm, things had fallen apart. He didn't know how much time had gone by exactly. It was too late when he tried to save the place. He knew it wouldn't work anyway. He wasn't a good manager. He wasn't his father. And he no longer had Laura to help him. The farm had been failing for years, but he'd hidden the information from Laura. If he'd told her maybe they could have saved the place, but his life was built on bad decisions.

And treating Jason as if he didn't belong and wasn't part of the family was one of them.

"Mr. Kendall," a familiar voice spoke to him.

Sheldon looked up. "Good morning," he said. Audrey Thompson stood in front of him. She was a small woman, slightly overweight. He was fifty-one and he estimated she, too, was probably in her early fifties. She spoke to him daily when she walked along the marina. It was part of her exercise program she told him. Audrey was raising her grandson. Her daughter, a single mom, died after her car was struck by a drunk driver when the child was six. He was nine now.

"You're out in the heat, I see," Sheldon said.

"The North Carolina sunshine can be unforgiving. The camp bus was a little late, and

I had to get to the post office. How are you this morning?"

She asked the same question every day he saw her, which was usually Monday through Friday. "I'm managing," he answered her as he always did.

She waved then and kept walking. Sheldon watched her go. He was impressed with how she doted on her grandson. She was patient and caring. Sheldon had often seen them along the water. Audrey mentioned she was a schoolteacher and had the summer off, so she had the days to tell the boy about the sky, the clouds, the sea, sea creatures, the sand. Sheldon even heard her explaining how glass was made from sand. He was surprised to learn the process himself.

It was amazing the things he didn't know and had never been interested in before. But what was more amazing was watching the way she treated her grandson with kindness and love. His father had never treated either him or Jason with the sort of care Audrey bestowed on her grandson. Sheldon had been cloistered in his father's narrow-minded world. Sheldon was glad to see how other people lived and how they looked after one another.

When noon came, Sheldon knocked off for lunch and headed home. Along the beach were a series of cheap but cheerful bungalows that could barely be called houses, but that's what they were for some of the lower-income families in the community. Sheldon lived in one of these cottages that he rented from a man in town. The summer was sweltering, but this past winter, when he'd arrived in Meadesville, and taken the cottage, the winds had blown in off the Atlantic and swirled around the estuary freezing his fingers and feet. He longed for his warm bed back in Maryland. But that was no longer his and would never be again. Sheldon didn't want to see the place where he had been born and raised go to strangers. He wondered what it was like now. When he'd left the Kendall, the main house was no longer the pristine white color with black shutters it had been before his father died. When Sheldon was locked out the grass was overgrown, the paint was peeling and there were several leaks needing repair. The barn was empty and Sheldon owed thousands of dollars for feed, repairs and services. He had every cent he owned—$208.76—in his pocket when he was evicted.

That hadn't taken him far and he found himself doing things only Jason would do. He hated Jason more then. Irrationally, he knew his predicament wasn't Jason's fault, but Jason would think nothing of hitchhiking, digging ditches, working on road crews or taking refuge at a homeless shelter. It was beneath Sheldon. He thought he would never do anything like that.

But he had.

He'd done that and more. When he couldn't find a soup kitchen, when he was too far from anyplace, when he had no more money, he scoured trash cans, looking for anything to eat to stay alive. Now he had a job and a place to live. His pay was a little more than minimum wage. He had no savings and usually cooked and ate his own meals—simple ones, nothing fancy. His bathroom had no mirror in it, so he didn't always know what he looked like, but the last time he saw a reflection in a store window, he seemed identical to his father if his father was a fiftysomething vagrant. He had a beard and unkempt hair. He'd lost at least forty pounds and wore thrift-store finds.

He no longer resented Jason. Jason was a survivor. He would adapt, do what was necessary to get back on his feet. Sheldon used his brother, no longer thinking of him as a half brother, as an inspiration. Every time he wanted to quit the menial job, he considered what Jason would do. Jason would stick it out. He'd perform the tasks at an exemplary level until he raised enough money to move on. Then he'd go to the next job. Sheldon was a Kendall, and while Jason was also a Kendall, his half brother had a tougher bloodline on his mother's side. It had made him strong. Surely Sheldon could at least do half of what Jason would do.

Again, he stopped to look over the marina and speculate where Jason might be. Had leaving the farm destroyed any love he had for the Kendall? Would he ever return? Sheldon was hardly in a place to know. He didn't ever expect to see the Kendall again himself. Knowing it was no longer in his family, yet being nearby, would be too much for him.

He'd disappointed his father and the generations of Kendalls that had come before him.

He would not go back.

In his bungalow, Sheldon set a small pot in which he'd dumped a can of soup on the burner and waited for it to heat. Even though the temperature outside was nearing the century mark, he lunched on soup and bread, saving his dinner for the larger meal of the day. Tonight he was having canned chili with rice.

Sheldon ate leisurely and alone. When he finished, he cleaned his dishes, set them in the drainer for use later and took a quick shower. He changed clothes and headed back to the cabin cruiser he was working on.

"Whatcha doing?" Christian Mitchell, Audrey's grandson asked.

Sheldon looked down to find the nine-year-old standing next to him. He wore gray shorts and a white shirt with an anchor on the breast pocket. His feet were in deck shoes and no socks. Sheldon had met the boy several times and he always came to talk to him. While Sheldon wasn't used to small children, he thought Christian missed male company.

"Cleaning the bottom of the boat," Sheldon told him.

"How'd it get dirty?" he asked.

"These things are in the water and they see the boat and they want to make it their home."

"So?"

"They slow the boat down when it's sailing and you know how much we all like speed."

Christian smiled. He'd seen Christian on his bicycle and knew if his grandmother found him riding in places this far from their home, she'd ban any use of the two-wheeler.

"If we don't get the barnacles off, they'll eat right through and then the boat will leak. We can't have that happening."

Christian was shaking his head slowly from left to right. "Then the boat would sink. And it they couldn't swim, they could drown," the child said.

"That's right."

"Can you sail?" Christian asked.

"No," Sheldon told him. As far as his work was concerned, he hoisted the boat out of the water and worked on it while it was either in dry dock or he'd swing it over the wharf and work on it there. He was doing that today.

"How come you work on boats then?" Christian asked.

"A man's gotta eat," he said.

"You eat these?" The child's face squinched up as he peered at the barnacles on the tarp and his expression was that of horror.

"No, I don't eat these," Sheldon mimicked with a laugh.

The child looked relieved. "They're ugly," he said.

"That they are," he agreed. He glanced farther down the marina and then by the row of houses leading away from the area. He didn't see Audrey. "Does your grandmother know you're here?"

Christian stared at the ground, but didn't say anything at first. "I told her I was going to play video games."

"Here, by the water?"

He nodded, but Sheldon could see there was little belief in the gesture.

"And what did she say?"

"She told me to be home in time to eat."

"And that's all she said?"

He nodded.

Sheldon stopped working and stooped down to Christian's level. "I know you like the boats, Christian," he said. "I know you like coming here, but your grandmother could be very worried if she can't find you where you're supposed to be. Do you understand?"

He nodded again, but still refused to make eye contact with Sheldon.

"Tell you what."

The boy looked up as if he was about to get a reprieve.

"Why don't you go tell her where you are. And if she says it's all right, you can come back."

Christian smiled. He ran off, calling his grandmother.

Sheldon watched him go. He smiled after the boy, his gangly legs trying to keep up with his growing body. At least there was one person who liked Sheldon for who he was. Christian didn't mind being around him. He didn't look at Sheldon's clothes, his beard or where he lived and judge him as someone unworthy of his attention.

Suddenly Sheldon remembered Jason. He was about Christian's age when he came to live with them. Had Jason been as innocent and in need of love and acceptance as Christian when he came to the Kendall?

HOW HAD ALL this happened, Jace asked himself. How could Sheldon let the house and the horses go? He knew his brother loved the Kendall. Had the years changed him? Jace needed to know. He needed to understand what motivated Sheldon to give up and walk away, leaving everything he owned behind.

Why hadn't Sheldon tried to contact him? Of course, Jace had left angry over Laura, but when things had gotten so bad that Sheldon needed money, why didn't he at least call him? Sheldon could have tracked him down. Yet, just as his brother ignored him when he was present, he also cut him out of what he might have been able to provide to keep the farm in the family. As distant as Sheldon thought Jace was, the two still shared a bloodline and a heritage.

Questions, Jace thought. Since he'd arrived at the Kendall that rainy night all he had were questions and no answers. He was going to have to face facts and find his brother. Sheldon held the key to whatever was going on.

Jace wasn't even sure if Sheldon was still alive. His search for his brother, who was older than Jace by more than two decades, would have to start at square one. It wouldn't be easy. Yet someone had to know what had happened to him. Kelly said she thought he'd left the state. Why would he do that? He'd lived his entire life in Maryland. At the Kendall. Obviously, he had friends, business acquaintances elsewhere, maybe he'd gone to one of them? Jace wished he'd known his brother better, it would give him a clue now as to where to look.

All Jace could remember about his brother, other than their arguments, was that Sheldon was always at the farm and rode horses. Well, he certainly wasn't here any longer, and apparently he'd left with only the shirt on his back.

THE SUN WAS relentless on Meadesville. Sheldon scraped the bottom of a boat, one of many he'd be attending to at the yacht club that day. It was only nine in the morning and already his shirt was crusted with salt-laden perspiration. The wire brush he was using had seen better days, forcing him to scrub harder to get the pesky crustaceans off the surface. Would anyone back at the Kendall believe that he would be doing this kind of work? The irony was staggering. First Sheldon had lost his precious family home and now he labored for the rich locals. To think that Sheldon had once looked down on his half brother. He'd always called Jason his half brother when he deigned to talk to him or of him. Now he understood.

Sheldon stopped scraping and stood up. His back hurt and his fingers were cramped. He looked out at the marina. Sailboats, cabin cruisers, watersport and racing boats stood majestically in the sunlight. He hadn't been in Meadesville long. It was an affluent golf and boating community along the coast of North Carolina. The homes there were spacious and sold upwards of six and seven figures. They were newer than Sheldon's former home in Maryland but didn't have the history and time-honored traditions that the Kendall possessed. He'd been here for a little over eight months.

This hadn't been his destination when he left Maryland. Sheldon had had no destination, actually. He was lost, angry and without resources. Even his experience with horses was out of date for training them. He'd never trained a horse, technically, but lied and said he had. There were horse farms in Virginia. He'd stayed at a couple of them briefly, but being around them made him homesick for Laura.

He'd moved on and tried Kentucky, Pennsylvania, Virginia and West Virginia, but found no work. He couldn't remember how he got to North Carolina, only that he'd hitched a ride unaware and uncaring where the driver was going. All he knew was he no longer wanted to have anything to do with horses.

So he'd ended up in Albermarle. A man he met in a bar one night told him about a job and Sheldon followed up on it. He'd long since moved from believing he could find a management position on another horse farm. Apparently, his reputation as the former owner of the Kendall reached farther than he knew and no one would take a chance on him.

Lowering his expectations, he accepted the job maintaining the boats in the marina.

The work was hard, unyielding, usually enhausting.

He wouldn't complain. The old Sheldon would do nothing but complain, but this was a new world and he needed to adjust to it.

He prayed again that there was a little of Jason in him as he scraped the brush against the hull.

CHAPTER FIVE

SEVEN LONG AND very wide steps led to the porch of the big white house at the Kendall. Kelly stood as stiff as a statue next to one of the columns watching Jace stop his rental car in the circular driveway. She couldn't believe he was disrupting her entire life after only a few hours. Behind her stood his duffel bag. She was throwing him out.

He got out of the car, looking up at her.

"Where's Ari?" he asked. He probably thought her expression had something to do with his son.

"He's fine. He's taking a nap," she answered.

"Nap? Ari doesn't take naps."

Her brows rose. "Apparently, he does."

"What's wrong then?" He came around the car and looked up at her.

"As if you didn't know." She spoke through clenched teeth.

"I clearly don't understand."

Kelly knew he was lying. Color crept up his cheeks turning his face to a beautiful shade of crimson. Picking up the duffel bag, she tossed it down the steps. Instinctively his hands came out and he caught the bag.

"What's this?" He dropped it at his feet.

"You're fired, Mr. Kendall."

"Fired?"

"Yes, fired. I offered you room and board and to take your son in until you could get on your feet, and you repay me by going to the bank and trying to swindle me?"

She expected he'd drop his gaze, but he looked directly at her. While his eyes remained steady, she could see he was surprised that she knew about his trip to see Kurt Mallard.

"This is a small town, Mr. Kendall. Didn't you think word would get back to me about your *adventures*?"

"Actually—"

"Actually, you didn't," she finished for him. "So don't go behind my back and try and usurp my right to be here. *You* are the one who's trespassing."

"I know that's how it looks."

"That's how it is."

"Okay, okay," he said, raising his hands in defeat. "I could tell you I'm just surprised to find things so changed."

"What did you expect? That the world would stop until you returned here to set it in motion again?"

"For the Kendall, that's how it's been for a century." He paused and looked at the house behind her. "My father and my brother kept things the same. Tell me, when you took over this place, you didn't have to upgrade and re-store everything?"

Kelly shifted her weight from one foot to the other. That's exactly what she had to do. She'd spent a fortune bringing the house up to code. A lot of which she'd had to learn and then qualify to do herself, since she couldn't afford to hire professionals.

She'd put up with the dust and general mess of renovation by using the rooms not being worked on, until it was their turn, and she'd switch to living in the finished ones. It was a long, arduous process.

"Almost everything. And all right, most of what you said is true. But whether it is or isn't, you still have no claim here, and no business trying to undermine me. And what possible hold could this place have for you when you were treated with contempt by both your father and brother?"

Kelly watched him force himself to relax. "I see you know more about me than I thought."

"People talk," she said. "It's still a small county."

Jace moved up the steps and sat on the top one. He glanced at Kelly. After a moment she sat a discreet distance from him. She was angry, a body singing anger, yet she could feel the vibes that seemed to bounce off Jace.

"I never thought this place would or could hold anything for me," he began. He spoke softly as if he was talking to himself and not to an audience of one. "Then I got Ari."

"*Got* Ari?"

"He's adopted."

"You told me," Kelly said. "But you made it sound as if he was left on your doorstep."

"Close," he said. "His mother threw him to me. Ari is four. I've had him for three years."

"He wasn't an orphan?" Kelly asked.

"Not at first. He had a mom. I didn't know her. I only learned about her after she died.

I knew nothing about the cocaine factory where she worked." He stopped. "You're probably thinking a factory is a building. It's not. It's a hole in the ground, protected by guys with guns. I was working on a water pipeline through one of the jungles and the cocaine factory was nearby. There were rumors about it, so I knew it was there and our crews steered clear of it. But then it was raided. People were screaming and running in all directions when it exploded."

Kelly's heart went out to the small child sleeping in the bed upstairs.

"When we heard the bang, I ran toward it, grabbing and pulling people out of the wreckage. Ari's mother crawled out, dragging the child with her. She pushed him at me just as a second explosion rocked the ground. Both Ari and I went down, but I fell on my back instinctively keeping him safe. He's been with me ever since."

This, Kelly knew, was designed to gain her sympathy. It did, but she was determined not to show it. "And Ari is the reason for the return?"

"In part. Ari needed better doctors. I mentioned his asthma."

"You have health insurance?"

"I have to check on my options. I'm not sure anymore."

"What happens then?"

"I hope to have a job by then."

"I'd like to suggest that you put your efforts into finding employment with insurance instead of trying to get a bank loan to buy the Kendall. It's not for sale."

"I suppose that's fair. In the morning, I'll look for another place for us to stay."

"Dad?" The door to the Kendall had been ajar and Ari pushed it fully open and stepped onto the porch, his fist wiping sleep from his eyes.

Jace automatically opened his arms and the small child walked into them. He settled the still-sleepy boy on his legs.

Kelly's heart softened. She hadn't known Ari twenty-four hours, yet she felt protective of him. She loved how father and son cared for each other.

"For the sake of Ari," she began. "The job is still open. It has medical insurance. You'll be covered as soon as you sign the papers."

"I accept," Jace said without hesitation.

"However," Kelly stopped him. "If I even

think you're trying to undermine me in any way, I'll throw you off the property and you can fend for yourself."

She refused to include Ari in that threat.

Though Kelly's anger had abated, she was still unnerved. It had been a while since she was intrigued by a man the way she was with Jace, even as he stood wet and lost in her foyer the night before.

To send him packing might have been the right thing to do, but she wanted to explore these other feelings. Even though getting the Kendall to be self-sustaining was number one on her priority list, she felt he could help her and she could work out the chemistry that was obvious between them.

"Wanna go for a walk, Ari?" Jace spoke.

"Wow! Yeah," he said, raising his head from Jace's shoulder.

The two got up and moved down the steps.

"Kelly, wanna come?" Ari asked.

She looked at the child, then at Jace. "I have a lot to do," she said. "Why don't you and your dad spend some time together?"

Jace nodded and he and Ari headed out. She watched them go, Jace holding securely on to Ari's hand.

They were a pair, Kelly thought. She couldn't imagine them separated, couldn't think of them ever being anything except father and son. She wondered if Jace was giving Ari the childhood he'd wanted. That this was the real reason he'd returned to the Kendall. She didn't doubt that the child probably needed to see a specialist. But she thought that could be the secondary reason he was at *this* farm. He wanted Ari to know the love and support of a father that Jace had wanted and never received. He wanted Ari to be on the land where he'd grown up and know that he could always call it home. That this was his heritage and that love and understanding were his.

Kelly shook her head, trying to clear away the confusion she felt at the man and boy and their dependence on one another. Their love was obvious. She couldn't fault them for their feelings. It was her own feelings that bothered her. *She* owned the Kendall. And she was not giving it up. It wasn't her duty to solve Jace's problems. She couldn't go back in time and fix all the things his father had done or not done to him.

The Kendall was hers. And as she told him, it wasn't for sale.

ARI LET GO of Jace's hand and started running across the grass. His short little legs carried him toward the far fence where Kelly used to sit and watch the horses. Jace didn't take any notice of her back then. Usually he was riding to try to get the hurt out of his system. All he could remember was her red hair, which even on a dark and cloudy day was still noticeable. Ari seemed to go straight for that area. Jace followed him.

The fence had been replaced and painted a bright white. It would reflect off car lights in the dark and act like a beacon leading to the house.

Jace shook it, checking its sturdiness. Kelly said she'd done a lot of the labor, but he couldn't imagine her digging fence posts and resetting the miles of fencing that surrounded the farm. The fence, however, was solidly set. He lifted Ari and placed him on the top rung. With his arm around the boy, he looked over the grass toward the eastern slope of the property's pasture.

Jace had some savings. He could make a

down payment on a small house and support Ari, but he needed to be available for engineering jobs that might take him away from the boy, whereas Ari needed stability. And Jace didn't want to relinquish his stake at the farm, although he'd never really had one. Somehow he was going to have to get Kelly to let him buy it back.

"Do you think we could get a horse, dad?" Ari asked.

"Can you ride?" Jace raised his eyebrows as if he was surprised at the question.

Ari smiled and looked embarrassed. "I bet Kelly knows how to ride. She could teach me. Can I ask her?"

"May I ask her?" Jace corrected.

"May I ask her?" he repeated.

"We don't have any horses now, Ari, but when we get some, I'll be sure to teach you to ride."

"Wow!"

Jace wondered it Ari liked it here or if he missed his home country. The child had never known anything except the small village he'd been born in.

"Ari, are you enjoying it here?"

"Yeah. Did you see my room?"

Jace nodded. "I mean do you miss home?"

"You said this was gonna be our home." His voice sounded frightened, as if he'd been promised something and someone was about to take it away from him.

"You had a lot of friends there. Here there's no one. At least, not yet."

Ari's eyes filled with tears. "Are we going back?"

Jace put his arms around him and lifted him off the fence. He cradled him close as the child sniffed. "We're not going back."

"You promise?"

"I promise."

Small arms circled Jace's neck. He didn't know what it was about the Kendall that had gotten to Ari, but it had happened quickly. The only thing Jace could think of that had gotten to him was a person…not a thing. And that same person was the current owner of the Kendall.

SATURDAY NIGHT, SHELDON THOUGHT. He didn't work weekends since the owners of the boats usually took them out on Saturdays and Sundays. He enjoyed the rest. He read at night since he had no television, radio or phone.

They were luxuries he'd discovered were unnecessary. And there was no one to call even if he had a phone.

He spent most of his free time at the library. At least he had a library card and he never returned books late. The librarian always smiled at him, although he knew she pitied him. His taste in books was eclectic. Sheldon wanted not only to be entertained with the fiction he read, but he wanted to learn, to study subjects that interested him and on those he thought he needed to know.

He'd taken many books out about boats and the creatures that attacked them, the sea tides, the North Carolina coastal region, cook books and electrical wiring. He didn't know why he took the electrical wiring book out. The bungalow was dimly lit, its electrical panel decades old.

Tonight Sheldon was reading an engrossing novel about a female clock maker. He heard the soft lap of the water not far from his front door. Sheldon loved the water. He'd lived with horses all his life and never knew how soothing the water could be. He went back to his book, pulling it closer to his face so he could see the print.

A knock on the door startled him. No one had knocked on his door since he rented the bundalow. Who could that be?

Sheldon untangled his long legs and stood. The knock came again. Slowly he made his way over and peered through the window. Christian stood there.

"What are you doing here?" Sheldon asked as he yanked the door open. It wasn't dark yet, but it was dangerous for the boy to be alone.

"My grandma sent me to invite you to eat with us."

"What?"

"We want you to eat with us."

"Oh."

"You should come. We're having meat-loaf." Christian frowned at that. "I'd rather have a hamburger, but Grandma says we can't eat hamburgers every day."

"Did you know meatloaf is hamburger? It's just presented differently. I bet if you put yours on a hamburger bun, it would taste the same."

"Do you think so?" His smile was wide and his eyes open in anticipation.

"I'm sure of it, but—" He stopped, raising

a finger and making sure he had the child's attention. "You'll have to eat all your vegetables." Sheldon felt slightly foolish giving a child advice about what he should eat since his own diet consisted of whatever was cheapest.

"So, are you coming?"

Sheldon hadn't had a home-cooked meal in years. His stomach reacted to the thought of some delicious meatloaf. He wanted to go, but he also wanted to be presentable and he had nothing that would make him look like the man he used to be.

"Give me a minute to clean up," he said. "You wait there."

Sheldon quickly washed his face and brushed his teeth. He pulled a clean, though unironed shirt from his closet and slipped into it. His shorts and deck shoes would have to do. Soon he joined Christian on the sand and they walked the short distance to the house that the boy and his grandmother occupied.

"Good evening," he said formally. "Thank you for inviting me." He stood stiffly and uncomfortably. He was unsure what to do or say and where to put his hands. He had nothing to bring her, no wine, no flowers, no candy.

"Come in. The food is hot and ready."

Christian jumped right into his seat. Sheldon looked confused as to which chair he should take. Christian pointed at one of the chairs and Sheldon took it, assuming the other one was his grandmother's. Audrey slid in front of the final place setting.

"Grandma, Sheldon said if I put my meat on a bun, it would be a hamburger. Can I do that?"

"May I do that," she corrected in what must have been her best schoolteacher voice. "And if you want a bun, you can have it."

"But I'll have to eat the vegetables, too." He presented it as a statement, but it was really a question.

"Yes, young man." She made him a plate and set it in front of him with meatloaf, mashed potatoes and summer squash. Then she got up and a moment later set a hamburger bun in front of him. The boy smiled and took it, proceeding to lift the slice of meatloaf and put it on the bread.

"Would you like a bun, too?" she asked Sheldon.

"No, thank you."

She took her seat again. The smell of the food was making his mouth water. Sheldon hadn't seen so much food in one place in a long time. And it was simple food. Not pheasant, coq au vin or arroz con pollo. Yet it looked like a feast to him.

She piled his plate with large portions. Instead of a bun, she added biscuits and checked with him to see if he wanted gravy on his potatoes. Sheldon nodded. When she passed the plate and they bowed their heads in prayer, he was truly thankful.

He wondered if she pitied him, too, if his thin body had triggered this invitation. Sheldon didn't bother to analyze it too closely. He was hungry and he was going to eat as if he appreciated every single mouthful.

And he did. He'd never appreciated food as much as he did tonight.

A COUPLE OF days later the heat and humidity had given way to comfortable weather. Sheldon walked into town. He was low on supplies and needed to replenish his stash of canned goods. After having dinner with Audrey and Christian, he longed for better food, but he couldn't afford it. He carried a basket so he wouldn't make the mistake of buying more than he could comfortably carry. It was a mile back to the marina and only once had he barely made it with the bags he was carrying.

Picking up some fresh carrots and broccoli, he knew he could eat them raw or with a little salad dressing. He stood in front of the bottles of dressing debating whether or not he should spend the money on one. He didn't really need it. Deciding against it, he turned. Audrey stood at the end of the aisle and was now coming toward him.

"Hello," she said, her voice both surprised and happy.

"I was just doing a little shopping," Sheldon said.

She glanced at the basket in his hand. He was glad to have chosen the fresh vegetables.

"I don't need much," he said to explain so few items in his basket.

Audrey nodded as if she understood, but Sheldon knew she didn't. How could a woman with a decent salary understand his needs for the bare necessities of life. It was why he kept to himself. He didn't want to have to explain his life or his lifestyle. And he didn't want charity. It wasn't that it was beneath him. Sheldon had eaten at homeless shelters and accepted handouts when he had none.

But he was standing on his own feet now. He had a job, however humble. And he did for himself. Not even Jason would have thought he could survive in a world outside of the Kendall. But he was proving him wrong. Even if Jace didn't know it.

"I want to thank you for dinner the other night. I really enjoyed it."

"It was my pleasure. I hope you'll come again."

"I can't," he said. The words were out before he could stop them.

"Why?" she asked.

Sheldon searched for the right words.

"Is it because of the food? Something you don't like?" Audrey asked.

"The food was delicious. The best I've had in a long time," he assured her.

She smiled. "Does it have anything to do with Christian?"

"He's a wonderful child and I enjoy being around him."

"Then what is it?" Audrey asked.

"It's hard to explain. I can't tell you about it now."

"All right," she said, but she didn't give up. "How about you tell me about it as I drive you home?"

Sheldon looked confused.

"My car is in the parking lot. As far as I know, you don't have one and it's a long walk back to the marina."

"I like to walk," he said.

"Oh, stop being a martyr and accept help when it's offered."

Sheldon smiled at that. "I'll meet you at the front door."

CHAPTER SIX

THE FIRST-FLOOR office that Kelly worked out of faced east. She'd removed the pocket doors and installed french doors in their place. It allowed the light to flow out into the hall and make the space brighter.

It was her policy to review the business every morning at seven. Using her project-management skills, she would study the expenses of the ongoing renovations and the future plans for making the property an income-producing concern. If all went according to her projections, the Kendall Farm Restoration Corporation would come into fruition. She'd been distracted for the past two days with Jace and Ari. But she was back on schedule now. She'd asked Jace to meet her at nine so he could sign all the employment papers and she could give him a list of things that needed his attention.

Taking a drink of her coffee, she clicked on

the Kendall's financial details. Using the time to go over the books, she realized she was getting close to a zero balance in her account. She'd already mortgaged the place as much as the bank allowed. Thankfully, she had an advance check for $10,000.00 from a modeling agency that had asked to use the place for a week. When they finished their location shoot, she'd get the balance. The money wouldn't go far, but it would pay Jace's salary and help with some of the marketing she was doing. She'd contracted with local visitors' bureaus and had brochures being printed to announce the opening of the farm for visitors.

She'd worked with a web designer and the site was ready to go live. There were more details that needed coordination, but she was on schedule.

Kelly glanced at her grad school degree hanging on the wall. Her MBA got her a job at an advertising and marketing firm on Madison Avenue. In charge of several key product accounts, she was on her way up the ladder. Then disaster happened. She lost a big client. She winced at the memory of her client telling her they were switching to a rival firm. Nothing she said could change their minds. Nothing she offered was good enough. Afterward, she felt as if there was a cloud over her and no longer was she given the important clients. Advertising is a business based on image and perception. Kelly was good, but one failure was all it took to end her chances at being the golden girl.

When her grandmother died, leaving her a small inheritance, and the Kendall came on the market, Kelly snapped it up with the intention of proving her promotional skills were as honed as ever. Looking over the marketing plan, she made a few changes and hit the print button. As she pulled the page from the printer, Jace came in.

"Oh," Kelly said, startled as she turned back from the machine. "Is it nine o'clock already?"

"Afraid so," he said. He took a seat next to the desk. He held a sheath of papers.

"Are they completed?" she asked.

He nodded, handing them to her.

Kelly checked to make sure the insurance forms had no gaps. Finding none, she looked up.

"They seem fine. I'll submit them right away."

Placing them on the top of her inbox, Kelly looked over the pages on her desk. Rifling through some, she glanced at Jace. "I'm usually more organized than this," she said, finding what she was searching for. "Here's a list of things I'd like you to start on. I made notes about what needs repair and what needs to be replaced."

Jace looked at the list. He nodded several times.

"Anything else?" he asked.

"Yes. I was hoping you could let me know if you think of anything else that should be done or restored here at the Kendall, given your association with the place."

He sat forward in the chair. "What do you mean?"

"I've mentioned I've done a lot of the work myself, with my cousin's help and her husband's, but if I should bring in a specialist for something, let me know." She pulled another sheet of paper from her desk and handed it to him. "These are the projects I worked on."

"You did all these?" He scanned the long list.

"I did."

"Including replacing the fencing along the road?"

She nodded. "That's right."

"I'm impressed." He stood up. "I'll get going on those jobs that need doing." At the doorway he stopped and turned back. "Do you mind if I take Ari with me?"

"Not as long as you're responsible for his safety."

"Don't worry. He's always my first concern."

"I watched the two of you together," she said.

His eyes flashed.

Kelly felt a streak of heat run through her as if she'd just made a confession, that she'd somehow invaded the privacy of a father with his son. "I didn't mean anything by it, just that it's obvious how much you two love each other. I can tell you wouldn't let anything hurt him if you could possibly prevent it."

He gave his head a shake and left, but not before Kelly saw the bob of emotion in his throat.

CHAPTER SEVEN

KURT MALLARD HAD been right, Jace thought.
The sunlight shining through Kelly's hair
was like watching a beautiful fire. It mes-
merized him. He couldn't take his eyes off
it or her. Outside he perused her list and decided which tasks to complete first. With Ari
trailing behind him, he strengthened barn
door fittings, checked to see that the correct
size stone for the added pathways had been
delivered, put up a half dozen shelves in the
garage and reorganized the storage there. It
took him two days to complete just the first
third of the list. As he went about his work,
to say that he was impressed with everything
Kelly had done would be a gross understate-
ment. Jace could see her presence at the Kendall was more than an asset.

Jace knocked lightly on her office door
with Ari standing next to him. She invited
them in. Jace held the list up. "I've done a

few things. Thought you might like a status update." He handed her the paper, which he'd added columns to. There were check marks in red indicating the tasks he'd completed, the date they were completed, what was decided on and finally his initials under the approved column.

She looked at it, then up at him. "You're very thorough."

"Comes with the job," he said.

"I helped," Ari stated.

Kelly smiled at him, a smile she'd never given Jace.

"What did you do?"

"I held the light so dad could look at the... the..." He faltered.

"Joist," Jace provided.

"Joist," he repeated.

"I'm sure you were a big help," Kelly told him.

Ari beamed.

"Since it's the end of the day, I thought I'd finish that library for you, but I see you've already done it."

"I plan to put the books back in another week. The paint needs time to really cure."

He nodded. "I'll start on the other things on

the list tomorrow. In the meantime, I promised Ari I'd take him into town. He hasn't seen anything of Windsor Heights, except the Kendall, since we arrived."

"You can come with us," Ari said.

"Yeah, you can," Jace imitated his son.

Kelly glanced at the spreadsheets on her desk. The office was full of unopened boxes. Jace noticed a brochure taped to one of them. One chair had several post office and courier boxes stacked, ready for tomorrow's pick up.

"You have to eat sometime," Jace prompted. He wanted to see her away from this place. She worked all the time, as if she had an impending deadline.

"Well, I suppose I can finish when I come back." She shuffled her papers together. "Let me freshen up. I'll meet you at the front door in five minutes."

Twenty minutes later they were sitting at the Hamburger Palace, a fast-food place where Ari was stuffing himself with a huge hamburger and a plate of french fries.

"Chew, Ari," Jace cautioned. The boy was shoveling food into his mouth as if he hadn't had a meal in days. "They don't have hamburgers where we were living," Jace told her.

"That must have been interesting. Living in a different country, I mean." Kelly took a bite of her burger.

"It was. I've lived in a few countries, actually. But, obviously, Colombia's meant the most to me." He used a napkin to wipe the side of Ari's mouth. "Too much relish."

"What did you do there exactly?"

"We put in a water treatment plant. It had just come online when Ari and I left."

"The job was over?"

"My part in it. The plant was completed, outfitted and online. The maintenance crew was in place and it was time for me to be transferred to another project. But I opted to return here."

He looked at Ari. Kelly followed his gaze and he knew she understood his meaning. She reached for the bottle of catsup and poured a little on the side of Ari's plate. Then she dipped a French fry into the sauce and offered it to him. Ari bit it.

"Mmm," he said, and picked up his own fry, repeating the procedure Kelly had shown him.

"Have you inquired about pediatricians, yet?" she asked.

"Before we left, I'd looked into some, but I haven't visited them. Would you know of any?"

Kelly shook her head. "I've never been around children or anyone with children, so I can't help you there. But I'm sure there are services you can call to inquire about specialists. You can use the computer to look up the types of doctors who are part of the insurance plan."

Again he looked at Ari. "It's amazing that since he's been here, he hasn't had a single episode." He shrugged. "I think he's happy."

"Many people with asthma live without episodes," she said.

"Ari used to have them regularly."

Hearing his name, Ari paid attention to him. "I have my inhaler," he said. His hand went to his pocket to prove it.

"I know you do," he said.

"I never go anywhere without it." Ari was shaking his head and speaking slowly, the way Jace had spoken to him when he was old enough to understand that he needed the inhaler to help him breathe.

Jace smiled and Ari tucked it in his pocket before returning to his food. Turning back to

Kelly, Jace looked at her hair. It was loose and flowing down her back. He wanted to run his hands through it, but she was his employer and he couldn't do anything to jeopardize that. He needed the job in order to keep the insurance.

"I need a favor," Jace said. He changed the subject to take his mind off Kelly's hair.

"What is it?"

"I have to return the car. I hoped you could find it in your schedule to follow me to the airport and bring me back to the Kendall?"

"I forgot it wasn't yours. Of course, I'll drive back and forth. I can drop off some of the brochures I have along the way."

"Brochures?"

"It's one of my marketing ideas to get the Kendall to be self-sustaining. It's been a lot of hassle, but I think it'll be well worth it."

"What's that?"

"I've negotiated a deal with the Maryland tourism people to include brochures in all those places that people stop along the highway. When I go to the airport we'll pass right by the tourism offices. I can deliver the brochures."

Jace remembered the boxes in her office. "Why?" he asked.

"Why what?"

"Why are you distributing brochures for tourists?"

"Oh." She smiled widely and leaned closer to him. "I'm opening the house for tours."

"What!" Jace recoiled. "You can't."

"You forget," she said. "I own the Kendall."

AFTER EATING DINNER with Jace, Kelly was having second thoughts about him staying on at the Kendall. He came with baggage, lots of it. She knew it when he arrived, but she'd misjudged how much he could interfere with her plans. He'd grown up on the farm and was having a hard time thinking of it as belonging to anyone except him or his family.

Ari was the one bright spot, but she wouldn't let her affection for the child obscure her vision. She was doing what had to be done if she wanted to not only live here but make the place successful again. She had to make Jace understand that. She'd worked through several plans and she'd had to discard most of them as not producing enough income to warrant the effort.

As soon as Ari was asleep, she'd asked Jace to come to the main living room. She had coffee set up on the small table and was prepared for the discussion. This was no different from the presentations she used to make when she was at her New York firm. Only this time she was speaking from the heart about something that had a lot of meaning for both of them. She was worried, too. If he didn't agree with her, their employment relationship could be over.

Kelly poured coffee into her cup and added cream. Jace's footsteps on the hall floor alerted her to his presence. Her heartbeat jumped and she took a long breath. He stepped inside the living room and stood there a moment looking at her. He'd changed his shirt, replacing the earlier short-sleeved one for a sweater.

"This is a pleasant room," Jace said. "I see the furniture has been changed. I like this better." He came forward and poured himself a cup of coffee. He drank it black and made a face at its taste.

"Isn't it strong enough?" she asked.

"It'll do," he said. He didn't sit, but carried it around the room as he appeared to inspect everything in sight.

"Should I apologize or should you make the coffee from now on?"

"I'm sure I'll get used to it over time."

Kelly frowned. "Time. That's what I want to discuss." Kelly stood up. "I mentioned that I have certain plans for the house. Plans you are opposed to."

"It did come as a surprise. I never thought anyone would want to let strangers into their home and have them roam around."

"They won't be roaming around. All tours of the house and property will be escorted." She waited.

Using both hands, despite the coffee cup, he signaled for her to continue. "I intend to open the house one day a week to tourists. I've hired a crew of college students who will be dressed in period costumes to provide the guided tours. As you know I've designed and printed brochures, and distributed them to tourist bureaus throughout Maryland and the four states that border it."

"Just for the record, don't expect me to don a costume and play lord of the manor."

"I won't, but I also expect that you won't get in my way."

He said nothing and his silence was irritating. Kelly decided to go on. "I also have plans in the works to help to attract events to the Kendall."

"Attract events?" He stepped forward and set his cup of coffee on a table. She couldn't figure out if he was closing his mind to everything she had to say. It didn't matter. She didn't need his approval.

"To begin, we have three weddings this summer. They will use the lawn for the ceremony and the ballroom and formal dining room for the reception. Photographs will be both inside and outside, weather permitting. There is a contract with a modeling agency in New York to use the Kendall for their next photo shoot. They will be here for three days, using the house and grounds to shoot an ad campaign for a fashion designer's upcoming collection. The library, garden, small living room and the red room will be used."

Stoically, he watched her without expression.

"I have a leasing agreement with Windsor Heights State College for their annual cotillion. It's scheduled for next November. In that case, we'll be using the grand ballroom, which will be decorated by the student committee and supervised by the dean of students."

"Whose idea was that?"

"Actually, it was the Windsor's. The social committee chairperson contacted me and I signed the agreement. We need the money and they are paying a hefty sum. Apparently, having a house that's been continually occupied since the Civil War is a draw for the college. In addition, some of the students are helping out with the much needed improvements. They will be on sight come September and receive a credit for their work. I would appreciate it if you would be the project leader on that if you're still here by then."

"You think I'm leaving?" The smile on his face could be a smirk. Kelly ignored it. She had to persuade him and she believed in laying her cards on the table. As a marketing executive, she always told her clients the truth. They appreciated it.

"I believe that you will do what's right for Ari. And for yourself. There's nothing wrong with that, but if my changes for this place become so abhorrent to you because you can't get it out of your head that the Kendall no longer belongs to the Kendalls, then you'll have to consider whether or not staying here is the right thing for you both, or you'll just disappear like you did five years ago."

She saw it in his eyes, knew it would happen. "You're a runner, Jace," she continued. "Whenever things don't go your way, you get on a horse and you run. When the horse can't take you far enough, you use a car or a plane, or an engineering job. So no, I can't be sure you'll be here in September or even if you'll be here in the morning."

No one liked to hear a character assessment of themselves that was anything other than glowing. Kelly had told him nothing he could grab hold of that was good about himself. But she wasn't sorry she'd said it. "I'll let you know if I'm planning to leave," he told her. "So go on. I can't wait to hear what else is coming."

Kelly glared at him. "When we begin generating enough income, I'm going to build a racetrack on the ten acres behind the horse barn. There we'll hold races and charge fees. There'll be a club house, stables and viewing stands. It's a long-term project. I don't expect to begin it for several years."

Jace listened attentively without any expression. Kelly finished and let her words sink in. His gaze swept around the room. He'd already commented on the alterations she'd made to it.

When his eyes settled on her again, he said, "I'll meet you partway."

"I don't get it."

"I'll act as project leader in September with the students. I'll work on anything you want, but when it comes to tourists traipsing through the house, I draw the line."

"You don't—"

He stopped her with his hands, palms out. "I won't prevent. I won't undermine. But I won't participate."

"Fair enough," Kelly said. They weren't at war, but she felt as if she'd won the first battle.

"One more thing," Jace said. "I'm not a runner. I had a good reason for leaving five years ago and an even better reason for returning now."

"I know you left because of Laura," Kelly stated. Windsor Heights was a small town and gossip about people at the Kendall was its stock in trade. He stared at her with eyes so hard they could have lasered her in two. "You don't know the half of it."

CHAPTER EIGHT

KELLY HAD JUST left her office for her daily trek to the mailbox when she heard the phone in her office ring. Rushing back, she answered it before the machine kicked in.

"Kendall Farms," she said. "How may I help you?"

"Kelly." The voice on the phone was upbeat and chuckling. Kelly's mouth dropped open and her eyes widened. Immediately, she tensed. Perry Streeter's was the last voice she ever expected to hear. Perry—her ex and former colleague—gave the impression that he was in your corner, when he was anything but.

"Perry," she said. "This is a surprise."

"How's it going out there with the nature and sunshine?"

"It's wonderful, Perry. How could clean air, growing grass and the good earth be anything else?" She couldn't begin to guess what he wanted. She hadn't talked to Perry since their scene at her New York apartment two years ago.

"I was wondering if we could get together soon."

"Why?" Deliberately, Kelly didn't offer anything else. She knew Perry liked his clients to talk. Often they had an idea for a campaign they were interested in and he said he didn't want to get in the way. Kelly knew better. He didn't really have a good sense of design, so he waited for them to tell him what they wanted. Then he could turn it around and act as if it was his idea.

"We haven't seen each other in a long while."

"Wasn't that what you wanted? If I remember correctly, you said we were done, over, needed to go our separate ways and find our own direction." She quoted him word for word.

"I'm sure we've grown wiser since then. It's been a couple of years."

"I've grown," Kelly said, leaving the unspoken sentence to imply that he had not.

"I have, too. I was thinking of taking a day

off. I could come see you. We could have lunch, get back to where we were before."

The nerve of him, Kelly thought.

"You know to me you were always special, the one who was different, who knew me better than anyone else."

Kelly couldn't vouch for that, but she could say she knew his type.

"What do you have in mind?" she asked, keeping the sarcasm out of her voice.

"I thought we could make a day of it."

"You mean you want to see the Kendall? Are you thinking of planning an event here for a client?"

"No, I'm thinking of you and I spending time together."

Again her mouth dropped open. Spending time in his presence was the last thing she would want.

"Perry, I'm very busy. I have an opening coming up and I can't afford to take any time away from preparations for that."

"Kelly, we know you have time to take a rest and get back to work the next day. The place won't fall apart if you take one day off."

"Sorry, Perry, but enjoy your day off."

She didn't wait for him to say goodbye or

to try to make arrangements for another day or time. Kelly was not interested.

Back in New York, they seemed the perfect couple—young, upwardly mobile with plenty of disposable income. But he found someone else and suddenly Kelly was no longer the woman he wanted to be with.

And now, after two years, he calls and wants to pick up where they left off. Did he think she'd put her life on hold, waiting for him to see reason and return to her? Kelly was the one who saw reason. Not long after that, she's lost her first big client and was ostracized within the firm. It wasn't too hard to figure out that being let go would likely be the next step.

Disillusioned with everything about her life, she'd started to think of how to make some much-needed changes.

When Mira called to tell her the Kendall was going to be sold for taxes, it was the final puzzle piece Kelly needed to change her life. No way would she go backward and start seeing Perry again. There was no need anyway. Returning to Perry would be like stepping down, going back in time and reliving a life she had no possibility of enjoying.

"What was that all about?" Jace asked from the door.

Kelly instantly felt a glow inside her. She turned and faced him. "Past history," she told him.

"Are you all right with it?"

She nodded. "Over and done with."

"Is that what brought you back here?" he asked.

Kelly looked surprised.

"I have ears, too. I hear things," Jace said.

"Like what?"

"Like you bought the Kendall because of a breakup with some guy in New York."

That was it in a nutshell, Kelly thought. Jace had been kind. He didn't say because some guy in New York dumped her. "That's not the entire story."

"Was that him?"

"It was. He wants to come down and spend the day with me."

For a moment, Kelly thought she saw Jace frown.

"Are you going to let him?"

She watched him closely. His body language didn't change, but he let his breath out slowly. Kelly couldn't say she didn't know why. Jace was attracted to her. Any woman knew when a man wanted to move to the next level. Only she couldn't. Not yet.

She shook her head. "Old news. No longer relevant."

CHAPTER NINE

"I CAME BY your office for a reason," Jace said. It wasn't to overhear Kelly's conversation. But when she began to talk, he had listened.

"What did you want?" Kelly asked.

"The back garden is unfinished. I wondered if you'd mind if I worked on it?"

"What are you planning to do?"

Jace knew Kelly was seeing dollar signs. Even the garden required plants, sand and dirt, bricks and cording. Some landscaping jobs cost thousands of dollars, but this one wouldn't.

"I've drawn up a design if you'd like to see it."

She smiled then. It was a bright, wide smile. Maybe the phone call was forgotten. Jace stepped inside the office and went to the small round conference table that sat near the window. He unrolled a single sheet of drawing paper. Kelly came over and sat in one of the chairs. Jace stood and leaned over her. Her hair was close enough to touch. Jace breathed in.

"This is beautiful," she said, showing the awe she must have felt.

The idea was simple in nature, a concept designed around a circle in a square. He'd drawn a large square with entrances on all four sides. The floor would be made of tile and outside the perimeter he'd place small shrubs of varying colors. They would change throughout the summer months. In the center of the square was a circle. In its center was a fire pit. Around the inside of the circle was seating. Walkways led to the fire pit that doubled as a table during warm weather. In another area he'd added a gazebo. It would be outlined with lights that would change color or remain constant on one color.

"What's this?" Kelly asked.

"It's a large table with chairs. I thought it would be a good place to breakfast on mornings when the weather permitted."

"That's a good idea. I love being outside. And it faces the house, so we'll get to see all the flowers that bloom in the summer."

"Have you determined a budget to go along with the plans?" she asked.

Jace produced another sheet of paper. It listed all the necessary materials and an estimated cost.

"This seems extremely reasonable," she said. "Are you sure you can do it for this?"

Kelly looked up at him and he didn't realize how close he'd moved to her. He was near enough to kiss her and that knowledge removed his ability to speak. All he could do was nod.

Their gazes held, then he moved a step back and the thread between them snapped.

"They're tearing down some old buildings along the highway. I made a deal with the foreman to take some of the debris they're throwing out."

"Is it any good?" She frowned.

He nodded. "It can be recycled."

She smiled then. "Save the planet. I like that."

"What about the plants?"

"There's a nursery not far from here that's going out of business. They're selling everything at huge discounts."

"How soon do you need the money?"

He dropped in the chair next to hers. "I don't need it all at once. The plants are the big thing. We don't want to wait in case everything is picked over by the time we need it."

She checked the cost breakdown again. "I think we can swing this," she said. "What is this line that says free?"

"Come with me." Jace got up and helped her out of her chair. He led her over to the window. His arm was around her waist before he realized it. He didn't remove it. It felt right to have it there. Her body was soft where he rested his hand on her hip.

"Look over there."

Kelly followed where he indicated. He couldn't tell how she felt about the physical contact between them. However, she didn't pull away. He took that as a good sign.

"See the horse stable?" he asked.

"Yes."

"Behind it and along the sides are shrubs."

Kelly peered at them.

"They're the kind that grow fast and replenish themselves. I plan to dig up the ones on the back side and replant them around the perimeter of the square."

Kelly turned and eased out of his grasp.

She returned to the table and looked at the drawing Jace had made.

"All right, you have my approval under two conditions."

"What are they?"

"If the costs are going to exceed this estimate, I need to know immediately."

"No problem. What's the second condition?"

"You'll be finished with this part of the renovation before the open house."

Jace nodded. "It'll be right under your window, so you get to see it each time you look outside."

There had never been a seating area there before, although Jace had once suggested it to Sheldon. Immediately, his brother rejected the idea. Jace had only remembered the notion when he saw Kelly at her office window. He did think the garden needed enhancing, but making the area appealing would please her.

And that pleased him.

SHELDON WASN'T ONE to talk openly about his feelings. He'd been on his own for years now and he was used to keeping to himself. Audrey, however, seemed to have other plans. He'd run into her or Christian at the oddest times and places. He hadn't told her his story, and she hadn't asked about it since that day in the grocery store.

Today he went for a walk along the beach and when he came to her house, she invited him in for iced tea. They sat watching the sea and Sheldon began to talk. He wasn't sure if he came for that reason or if he felt he needed to get the story out, tell someone about the way he had lived, provide the details of the rise and fall of a Maryland horse farmer.

"And that's how I got here," Sheldon said. Audrey had added a couple of sandwiches to the tray with their glasses of iced tea.

She'd listened carefully to him without saying a word. He told her of the jobs he'd tried and failed at. He told her about his father, how they treated Jason and that when his dad died, he totally cut Jason out of any legacy. He told her about Laura and how she'd died.

Once the words started to come, they poured out of him like the tides rushing for the shoreline. Sheldon relived it, seeing himself as the unlikable character he was, treating his brother so poorly. He saw himself as the bridegroom, in love with a woman who should never have been with him. He'd caused such pain to those he should have embraced. And now there was nothing he could do about it.

"What happened to Jason?" Audrey asked.

"I don't know. He left right after I married Laura. We didn't hear from him again. I know he was treated unfairly. At least I know it now. I don't forgive myself for my part in making him hate me. I couldn't have done a better job if I'd tried. And I tried. Whereas I should have known better."

"Don't beat yourself up," Audrey said. "You're no longer that man. You've grown and learned. You've traveled from Maryland here. Along your journey look how you've changed. The high and mighty person you say you were is gone. What I see is a compassionate man who cares about people."

"Now I'm the poor, humble creature who should have understood my brother better, but was unwilling to even listen to anything he had to say."

"We all make mistakes, Sheldon. Have you considered contacting the Kendall's new owners and seeing if your brother has been in touch with them?"

Sheldon had, but always found a reason not to do it. "It wouldn't be of any use for me to do that," Sheldon told Audrey. "Why would Jason want to see me or even speak to me. I'm afraid he's a bridge I burned long ago. There's no rebuilding it now."

"You may not be rebuilding the past," Audrey said. She spoke very slowly as if she'd taken a long time to think about her choice of words.

"In the past few years, you've moved around a lot, leaving behind what you don't want to face."

"I'm facing what I am," he said. "I know what I can't do and I know there will be no going back to the life I had."

"You need to resolve it," Audrey proclaimed. "It's hard, almost impossible, to go forward in life without resolving the past."

They sat in silence for several minutes. Sheldon had no watch. He'd long since sold it for food. He looked at the sun. He'd gotten used to being able to estimate the time by the movement of that heavenly body. He had a small calendar from a diner in his bungalow, so he could keep track of the days. Not that he cared much for them, but he needed to remember when to go to work.

What Audrey said made sense. It might be an exercise in futility, but contacting whoever owned the Kendall might give him some closure.

"What are you going to do now?" Audrey asked, interrupting his thoughts.

"Now?" He lifted one of the tea glasses. The drink was cool and seemed to refresh his throat after so much talking.

Audrey smiled. "I meant with the rest of your life. You've got a lot more living to do. Are you going to be cleaning hulls forever?"

"I have thought of becoming an electrician," he remarked.

"Don't you have to go to school for that?"

"No, but there is a test and an apprenticeship."

"Have you taken the test?" she asked.

Sheldon shook his head. "I checked some books out of the library and studied them."

"That's wonderful," Audrey said. "At the school where I work we have a technical maintenance man who's an electrician. Would you like me to introduce you to him so you can get first-hand knowledge of what's required?"

Sheldon was tempted to refuse her help, but that seemed like a foolish move. "I would appreciate that very much."

"Why an electrician?"

Farther alongthe beach, the marina was barely visible, but he could still see a glimpse of some of the sailboats moored there.

"Have you noticed all the lights on the marina at night?" he asked.

She nodded. "They make a pretty picture."

"I thought about them. I thought about a job that would always be needed. Someone has to fix those lights when they break down. Someone has to fix the electricity in all those big houses in town."

"That's a good reason," Audrey said.

Sheldon wanted something he could count on. He found he couldn't count on being the manager of a horse farm. The manual labor to clean the boat hulls would fall to a younger man in time. And he needed a profession that would pay him better than the minimum wage he was receiving now. The book on electricity seemed to jump out at him in the library and he'd checked it out.

He felt like he was making progress. He wouldn't go back, couldn't go back. That life was gone. But in this new life, he would try his hand at new things, be more open to people. Jason was an engineer, trained to be useful. He would never be hungry, never have to scrub scabs off boat hulls for the rich.

Sheldon had once thought his brother should be more like him, conforming to tradition, polished in his dress and manner. Those things were useless. And no good to him when everything went bad. Now Sheldon was planning to be more like Jason, resourceful and respectful. He might not be able to go back, and Jason would never know the effect he had on Sheldon, but Sheldon would know.

THE SMELL OF brewed coffee and bacon cooking woke Jace. Turning over he looked at the clock. It was just past seven. He sat straight up, realizing Kelly was up and that she'd been at her desk or holding a hammer or paint brush for hours already. It took him three minutes to shower and five minutes to dress. Ari was still asleep.

Jace was thankful the child no longer slept fitfully, which was why Jace probably overslept. He headed for the kitchen and the good-smelling coffee. Coming into the room, he found people he didn't know. A man and a woman.

"Hi," the man said. "I'm Drew." He offered his hand and Jace shook it. "You must be Jace."

"And I'm Mira, his wife and Kelly's cousin." She stood at the stove, ladling bacon onto a plate with a paper towel on it. "We heard you needed a car."

Jace just stared at them.

"Kelly called and said you had to turn in your rental," Drew said.

"We have a car that's not being used." Mira glanced at her husband. "And Drew is too stubborn to get rid of it."

"If I had, then Jace here wouldn't be able to borrow it." Drew looked back at Jace, the smile on his face told him the car wasn't a bone of contention between the couple. "It's not a car, actually, but a beat-up old truck. The keys are on the floor," Drew said.

"Thanks. I'll take care of it," was his reply.

"Good. Now, how about some breakfast?" Mira said. The mood brightened at the prospect of food.

"It smells wonderful." Jace helped himself and took a seat at the table. His plate was piled high with bacon, sausage, eggs and toast. A jar of homemade jam sat on the table. And the coffee she poured in his cup was exactly as he liked it.

"Kelly told me you like your coffee strong."

"This breakfast is terrific. Thank you. Where is Kelly, by the way?"

"She's up in the attic searching for some papers," Mira said. "She's already eaten. And Kelly is not one to let anything grow under her feet. She's always moving."

The three of them sat and ate their breakfast.

"What are you two doing today? Kelly mentioned you help her out around here, so I guess she gave you a list of things to do, too," Jace asked the couple.

Mira laughed. "Not today. We only came to deliver the truck."

Drew said, "I know your family lived here before, but when Kelly bought it, it was truly run-down. She's spent night and day bringing it back to where you see it today."

"It's a good thing the place was never protected as a historic landmark," Mira said.

"Why is that?" Jace asked.

"Rules," she said. "If the house or the grounds had been designated a landmark, there are hundreds of rules about what can and cannot be done. What materials can be used. Where things can be placed. Dimensions of buildings that can be built. And every change needs to be approved by a committee. It would have taken years for her to go through all the paperwork and inspections for even the most minor thing. Kelly has kept the character of the house, modernizing some of the areas that needed it."

Jace had forgotten his meal. Insight into the character of the woman he crossed swords with was more interesting.

Jace's respect for her increased dramatically.

JACE CLIMBED THE stairs to the attic. He'd had second helpings of breakfast and poured another cup of coffee. He was going to take it to Kelly as a kind of peace offering. Jace put everything on a tray and added a bud vase with a flower in it that he pinched from the arrangement on the foyer table.

The attic covered the entire house. It was

made up of several rooms, some finished, some not. As a young boy, Jace took refuge up there, before he'd found solace riding. When he first arrived at the Kendall, he'd hide and cry, missing his mother and not understanding why his father and older brother treated him like he'd done something wrong. That little boy came back to him as he reached the top step and opened the door to the first room. Inside there was faded wallpaper and old furniture haphazardly arranged or placed on top of other pieces. Closing the door, he went in search of Kelly. He found her in the next room. This one was clean of any dust and cobwebs. There were several pieces of furniture. Near Kelly was a round oak table half uncovered. Three chairs were around it, one with a broken leg, the other two without the spindles that used to be the back.

Kelly wore a short T-shirt and pants. This was what she wore most days. Her hair was in a long ponytail. It was set high on the back of her head and the way it swung when she moved reminded him of the combed and polished tail of a show horse. "Kelly. I brought you something to eat. Mira made this and it's delicious."

"Jace?" He could hear the surprise in that single word.

"I met your cousins in the kitchen. They said you were up here." He didn't tell her about the other stories they'd shared. He set the tray on top of a filing cabinet.

She took the cup of coffee and sipped it. "Thank you," she said. "What brings this on?"

"You did something for me. I thought I'd return the favor."

"What did I do?"

"Drew and Mira's truck."

"Oh, that." She brushed it aside as it meant nothing.

"Few people have ever done anything for me," he said. "I like to say thank-you when they do."

Kelly took the tray and set it on the table. Pulling a chair over, she took a seat and Jace did the same.

"Join me," she said.

He'd already eaten, but he took a piece of toast, tore off part of the crust and popped it in his mouth.

"Living here wasn't fun for you, was it?" she asked.

He shook his head, glancing toward the room where his sobs probably still echoed around the walls.

"That can change," Kelly said.

Jace looked at her. "It's in the past."

"For you," Kelly said. "For Ari, things can change for him. You can lavish all the love you want on him and things here at the Kendall will be different."

Jace realized she was speaking as if he was permanently stationed at the farm. When only a few days ago, she was telling him he was a runner and not likely to put down roots. But in everything that had happened, Jace knew Ari was at the top of his priority list. So he would do what was necessary to care for Ari and to keep him happy.

"I guess I should get to work," Jace said. "It must be time for my partner in crime to wake up, if he isn't already combing the rooms searching for me."

He got up and, taking Kelly's hands, helped her to her feet.

"Thank you for the food," she said.

He should have let go of her hands right

then, but he didn't. In fact, he didn't want to let her go at all. It was a totally foreign feeling for him, especially when she looked up and her eyes met his. They were big and questioning.

Jace had pulled her forward and brushed his mouth over hers before realizing he'd done it. When he saw what he'd done, he wanted to do it again. Wrapping her arms around his waist, he stepped even closer and kissed her full on the mouth. There was something between them. That undefinable something that only two people with a special connection understood. Her eyes opened slowly. There was a dreamlike quality to them.

"Jason…" she started, using his given name, which so few people used.

"I knew you weren't as indifferent to me as you'd led me to believe," he said, smiling. His voice was low and breathless.

"Please, Jason. I have a lot to do. A lot to contend with. I need to have my mind clear. I can't afford any complications right now. Please," she went on. "Don't confuse me."

CHAPTER TEN

KELLY PRACTICALLY RAN from the attic. She didn't stop until she'd reached the back porch. She was so confused. How could Jace have kissed her and how could she kiss him back? Why? she asked herself. Was she that transparent? He knew she was attracted to him. She could tell by the way he looked at her.

It seems every time she got near him something else happened. Kelly paced from one end of the porch to the other. She needed something to do. She needed to get her attention back on what was important. The Kendall was opening for tourists in two weeks. She was almost ready, but there were details still outstanding. She had to focus on the Kendall and *only* on the Kendall.

Her lists, she thought. They were in her office. She'd get them. They would tell her what she should be doing. Physical activity would help her get her mind off Jace.

And off the kiss.

She turned to go inside. Her heart jumped into her throat when she found Jace standing behind her.

"What is this?" he asked waving some papers at her.

She knew exactly what they were. They were the reason she'd been in the attic. She'd decided to give Jace what she had that his brother left. But him bringing her breakfast and sharing it with her had made her forget that purpose. After he kissed her, she could think of nothing except escaping his presence and his arms.

"These say that the Kendall hadn't made any money in years. That Sheldon mismanaged the place."

"You knew that," Kelly told him. Her voice was steady.

"I moved all those papers to the attic after I bought the place. Sheldon walked away with nothing."

"Nothing?"

"It was his choice. I never saw him. I told you that, as well."

"Why?"

"I don't know. Sellers remorse, whatever.

He no longer owned the place when I took possession. The county owned it. It was a tax sale. Sheldon was not required to be present, since his ownership rights had been severed."

"Where would he go? Why would he do that?"

"You'd be a better judge of his character than I would. All I know of him are the rumors and gossip I've heard. You lived with him. And, for the record, Jace, I'm not the bad guy here."

Kelly stood her ground. She would not be made to feel like the enemy.

"Listen, I have no ulterior motive in keeping information from you." She took a breath, hoping Jace would let his guard down, that his hurt and frustration would abate. "There are no locked doors in this house. You have free reign to look in any room you wish for information to help you find your brother. If there is something else you want, all you need to do is ask."

She watched as his shoulders dropped. Kelly wondered if his anger had really been about the papers he found or if it was the kiss they'd shared that spurred it.

"Jace." She took a step toward him, but she

was cautious; her heart seemed drawn to his yet she had to protect herself, and yes, Jace, too. "Ask yourself what you want to happen when you do find Sheldon."

BUILDING THE GARDEN with the adjoining patio and fire pit seemed like a good idea, Jace thought. He knew he could do it within the small budget he'd presented to Kelly. He also knew what it would entail engineering-wise. What he hadn't counted on was the tough resistance of the ground. This was something he should have taken into consideration when developing the proposal. But he hadn't.

Just as he hadn't thought about the repercussions of kissing Kelly in the attic. He'd been mad at himself, but he'd taken it out on her. Talking about Sheldon and how he'd lost the family's legacy had only spurred on his temper, misplaced though it was.

Since that day, he and Kelly had walked on eggshells, avoiding each other except where Ari drew them together. At first Jace had the garden to help him get over his emotion. Zealously, he dove into the process of clearing the land and preparing it. If Kelly hadn't mentioned the project to Drew, Jace would never have gotten the use of a backhoe and other equipment to dig the foundation. He'd have had to do it as a one-man work-army. The possibility of completing the spot under those conditions, before the open house, would be nil.

As it was, the garden would be done a couple of weeks before the *guests*—Kelly's word for paying visitors—arrived with their wallets and purses open. Ignoring the thought of strangers trampling the space, Jace switched his attention to Ari. His little helper was doing a wonderful job. Ari wore a small apron that the cook had made for him. Drew gave him some child-size gloves. He was working on clearing a patch of land that would be the fire pit area.

Jace checked the supplies stacked neatly by the back of the barn. Tomorrow they would begin the brick laying. As he turned back, Kelly was walking across the patio carrying a tray of lemonade. "You guys are working hard. I thought you might like a drink." She set a tray on a small table. There were chairs, but only Ari took a seat.

Jace was grateful that she was speaking to

him given how he'd behaved. He hated fighting with her. He hated not talking to her.

Ari immediately dropped his rake and ran over to get his lemonade. He drank deeply, then used his arm to wipe his mouth. Kelly handed him a napkin, but they all knew it was too late.

"How are things going?" she asked Ari.

"Good. We're going to start with the bricks tomorrow." He spoke happily and pointed to the stack waiting nearby.

She looked at Jace and he thought he saw something in her eyes, a small glint of attraction. He wanted to kiss her again. But restraint was a lesson he'd learned from a lifetime at the Kendall.

"Can we be friends again?" Jace asked, hoping Ari didn't understand.

She nodded. "I really wasn't holding anything back about Sheldon. I was trying to find the information for you."

"I know that now. I was just thrown off by the—" He stopped and shook his head.

The silence stretched between them. Then Kelly looked at the supplies. "Do you know how to lay brick?" she asked, the tension between them eased.

"Fine time to ask," he laughed, drinking his lemonade. "I do know how to lay brick. From the jobs I've done, it was necessary to learn many trades in order to complete a project."

Kelly would understand that, Jace thought. She'd already learned more than she ever thought she'd have to when she sat on that fence looking at the Kendall.

"I can't see what it's going to be. Except from your drawing," she said, surveying the expanse of yard they had cleared, "it's much larger than I thought."

Jace removed the gloves he'd been wearing and dropped them on the table next to the lemonade.

"Come with me," he said, offering his hand.

Kelly hesitated but then placed her hand in his larger one, Jace's fingers closed around hers. He felt the warmth of her fingers. Jace escorted her to the edge of the excavation.

"This is where the bricks will begin," he told her. "The inside will be tiled." He made a circle with his free hand. The other one still held on to hers.

Kelly didn't mind him holding her hand.

She liked it. It made her feel a variety of emotions she couldn't identify. She'd had boyfriends in her past, but none of them made her as breathless as the tiniest touches from this man at her side.

"The tile will go all the way to the circle Ari has cut out."

Hearing his name, Ari immediately looked up and smiled at her. "Great job, Ari," she said. "Well, so far it seems like everything is coming together."

"When it's done, and you look out that window—" he glanced at her office "—you'll have a beautiful scene below you."

"I'm expecting nothing less."

"Are we making too much noise for you to work?" Jace asked.

"I worked in a bull pen with people talking and shouting all the time. A few conversations and a hammer swinging now and then barely distract me."

Jace smiled, but said nothing.

"I'd better get back. More lemonade before I go?" she asked.

Ari held up his empty glass. Kelly filled it and refilled both hers and Jace's. All three of them drank.

"You're doing a wonderful thing," Jace said. His eyes were directly on her.

USUALLY KELLY DROVE the long driveway to visit the mailbox on the rural road. Sometimes she walked. Today was one of those days. Only riding a horse would be better than walking. She liked the return journey better, to come upon the Kendall in the stark sunlight, see the place as it was meant to be seen, grand, majestic and beautiful. She knew she was the only one who saw it that way anymore. It was the kind of vision that only a person who'd put her blood and sweat into it could feel.

Opening the mailbox, she grabbed the contents and shut the door. Rifling through the items, she found the usual magazines, advertisements for limited free gym memberships, bills and flyers inviting her to a complimentary dinner to discuss her retirement portfolio. She grinned at the thought. Right now she had barely enough money to buy lunch. Her retirement was hopefully far in the future and she'd have time to build up to it.

The last letter stopped her in her tracks. It was a plain white, business-size envelope, handwritten and addressed to the owner of the Kendall. Her name was not there. The return address was from Sheldon Kendall in Meadesville, North Carolina.

Kelly moved to lean against the five-bar fence. She stared at the envelope. It was addressed to her—she was the owner. But she knew whatever was inside wasn't for her. It was for Jace. Should she open the letter? Should she let Jace know that Sheldon was in North Carolina? Turning the envelope over, she stared at the blank backside for a long time. Whatever she decided to do, it would change her and her relationship with Jace. Not that they had a relationship, but Kelly had come to believe in him.

She'd made him part of the Kendall in her mind. But he wasn't. He had a life ahead of him. He had a son. And she didn't see him staying around the Kendall for the rest of his life fixing broken pipes and mending fences. The letter might be his ticket out of here.

On the other hand, Jace had told her that Sheldon treated him badly. Was this letter somehow a continuation of that? What would this letter tell him?

Kelly slipped her finger under the flap

and slid it along the edge. It opened and she pulled the single sheet of paper out and read it.

> *Dear Sir or Madam,*
> *I am the former owner of the Kend-all. I am trying to get in touch with my brother, Jason Kendall. I haven't seen him for years and have no idea where he could be. If he contacts the farm, would you please give him my address and ask him to contact me.*

It was signed, *Sheldon Kendall*. There was no phone number, only the address in North Carolina.

Kelly swallowed, placing a hand to her chest. Her heart was beating double time. It *was* him. It was really Sheldon. She knew where he was. And he was seeking Jason, wanted information about him, wanted to find him.

But what about Jason? He'd been angry with her once, mistakenly, over concealing information. But did he really want to suture the riff between them or did he want to start a fight over the loss of the Kendall? Would this information put Kelly in the middle of two feuding brothers? Would this mean the end of any hope for her and Jace?

She refolded the letter, taking her time given its value and importance. She slipped it back in the envelope and pushed it between two magazines. Then she began the return walk to the Kendall. Though, this time the glistening white structure growing larger before her wasn't what was on her mind.

"DON'T OPEN YOUR EYES," Ari said. "Keep them closed."

"I will," she agreed, taking a tentative step. The heat of the day hit her full-on as she left the air-conditioned comfort of the house.

Ari's small, clammy hand was holding on to Kelly's. Jace's hand was on the small of her back. The tender gesture didn't go unnoticed. The two of them were guiding her to the garden outside. It was finally finished and Ari and Jace wanted her to be surprised when she saw it.

Of course Kelly could see part of it from her office window, but she couldn't see the entire thing. And she pretended for Ari's sake.

"Wow!" Kelly exclaimed, using Ari's favorite word, as the blindfold was removed and she saw the garden. The wow wasn't just for Ari. The spot was beautiful. It was more than she thought it would be. "I love it," she said.

The two guys beamed. "Come look at this," Ari said. Taking her hand, he dragged her over to the seating in the center of the square. "Down here," Ari directed. Kelly went down on her knees. In the corner was a small tile that had the word *Ari* written into it. The handwriting was little more than chicken scratch, but it was readable.

"Ari, did you write that?"

He smiled widely. "Dad showed me how," he said. "But I wrote it. All by myself. Didn't I, Dad?"

Kelly twisted around to look at Jace. She raised her hand to block the sun.

Jace nodded to his son. "All by yourself."

"Where did you sign it," Kelly asked Jace.

"I'll show you," Ari volunteered. "He signed it twice."

"Once," Jace contradicted. "Over there near Ari's signature."

Kelly looked at him questioningly, then

turned back to the boy. Ari was pointing to a spot on the wall above his name. Jace bent near her and pointed. She looked and saw his name Jason Pharis Kendall. Kelly read it out loud. "Pharis?" She looked at him.

"My mother's maiden name."

He'd never told her about his mother. Only that he came to the Kendall after she died. Kelly put her hand on the carved letters. The tile was smooth, coupled with the depressions that formed his name. She felt as if she was touching him. Not the Jace he showed her, but the man he was inside. The vulnerable man who was capturing her heart.

THE EIGHT-YEAR-OLD Ford 150 ambled down the long driveway. Kelly's heart beat faster as she saw the truck coming. Jace was driving and he'd reach the Kendall's front circle soon. Ari stood by her, holding her hand.

Frowning, Kelly realized there was a horse trailer attached to the back of the Ford and he was pulling it toward them. Why would he need a horse trailer? They had no horses.

"What's he got?" Ari asked.

"I don't know, honey," she said softly.

Jace smiled and waved as he went by them

and continued around the house. Kelly didn't hear anything coming from the trailer, but her jaw dropped open when she saw the backside of two horses.

"Dad!" Ari shouted. Kelly kept a firm grip of him before he bounded down the steps in pursuit of the truck.

"We'll go around the back," she told Ari. The two went through the house and exited through the patio door. Jace had parked the truck and was opening the trailer.

Kelly let go of Ari's hand. He flew toward his dad. Kelly took a little longer.

"What is this?" she asked when she reached the pair. Jace backed a horse out of the trailer. It was a red mare. And she was beautiful. Kelly couldn't help admiring her color and the proud way she stood. Putting her hands on Ari's shoulders she held him a safe distance from the horse.

"I bought us some horses."

Kelly gulped. "You what?"

"We have a horse barn. This is a horse farm. We have to have horses."

Kelly wanted to react. However, she wouldn't argue with him in front of Ari. Her parents argued in front of her, usually about her father's drinking. Still Kelly knew how it made her feel. And while she wasn't one of Ari's parents, she wouldn't put him through that.

"Whose are they?" she asked, hoping she hadn't heard him say he bought them.

"Ours. They're for the farm."

"Wow. Really?" Ari said. "We can keep them?"

Jace nodded. His smile was wide. Ari squirmed out from under her and jumped up and down.

"We have a barn," she said, "but we don't have any feed."

"I bought some."

"On a continuing basis," she whispered. "How are we going to continue to feed them?" Kelly was living on the memory of money now. Her hopes were on the mansion opening in a couple of weeks. If they didn't make any money starting that day, she would be one step away from eventually defaulting on the mortgage loan. And Jace went and bought horses.

"We'll make it," he said positively. "How long has it been since you've been on a horse? Don't you miss it."

Of course she did. She smelled the animals and all the good feelings about riding came back to her.

"Is it okay, Kelly?" Ari asked. "We can keep the horses." He was so innocent and so positive.

Kelly looked at Ari and then at Jace. How could he put her in this position? She didn't want to disappoint the child, but she was practical. And it was impractical to house horses she couldn't afford to feed.

"I found a couple of saddles in the attic. I guess they were left behind when the horses were sold," Jace suggested. "Why don't you go for a ride?"

"Yes!" Ari jumped at the idea.

Kelly shook her head. She wasn't going to let him suck her in with a horse ride.

"Hold on to these." Jace handed her the reins. Kelly took them and Jace lifted Ari up and set the boy on the mare. The horse had no saddle. Jace looked at her. "You sure? I can bring the other one out."

She shook her head again.

He walked the horse several feet away, then turned in a circle, all the while keeping one hand on Ari.

"Kelly, you should come. This is fun." Ari laughed and kicked his feet, obviously like he'd seen someone on television doing.

"Don't do that, Ari," Jace cautioned. "We'll have to get you the right boots and saddle the horse." Ari laughed and Kelly thought her heart would burst.

IT HAD BECOME routine for Kelly to spend time watching Ari and Jace riding the horses from her office window. The horses became an unspoken addition. Jace kept them in feed and she didn't demand they be returned.

Lifting her cup, her arm hit the copier lid and it fell down. Kelly would swear it was closed when she left the office yesterday. She hadn't copied anything the day before. Maybe Mira or Drew had used it.

Turning back, she smiled at the antics of Ari and Jace. Jace got down from the horse and let Ari sit alone. He looked so small on the giant animal, but Ari wasn't afraid. He took the reins the way his father had done. And just as Jace had shown him, Ari moved with the horse, not against it. Kelly wouldn't say he was a natural. No one was. Everyone had to learn. She'd been around horses all her life and she knew no one took to the saddle on lesson one. But seeing the two of them every day proved that Ari would be an accomplished horseman soon.

Jace was good, too. She'd seen him ride, but since he bought the horses, he hadn't ridden them like he had when he was a wild teen. Kelly made a snap decision. In fact, she made two. Sitting her coffee on the desk, she opened her desk drawer and pulled the envelope out. The one she'd been hiding. Putting it in her pocket, she went to the closet and took one of the riding helmets. What Ari and Jace wore were the soft ones. They weren't going to do any serious riding, but they made sure Ari knew he needed to protect his head.

Moving quickly through the house and out the patio door, Kelly waved at the two guys and headed their way. Jace stopped and both climbed to the ground.

"Hi, Kelly. Are you gonna ride with us?" Ari asked.

"No," she said. She looked at Jace. "You dad is going to show us how well he can ride."

"What?" Jace looked confused.

Kelly offered him the helmet. "I know you

want to ride how you used to. With Ari, you can't, so Ari and I will stand over there." She indicated outside the fence. "And you can chase the wind."

A smile slowly split Jace's face. He hesitated only a second before exchanging the helmets with her. Kelly took the soft hat and reached for Ari's hand.

"Come on," she said.

The two of them walked to the fence. Ari's wiry little body slid through the slats. He propped his arms along the middle slat, while Kelly climbed over it. When they were safely out of any danger, Jace gave them a wave and took off. She and Ari watched as Jace flew across the field. He bent forward, lowering the wind resistance and rode as if he was the lead jockey in the Kentucky Derby.

"Wow," Ari said. He jumped up and down, taking tiny steps and clapped his hands. "Can I do that?" He didn't take his eyes off his father. Kelly didn't, either.

"Not immediately," she told Ari. "You have to get a lot taller and learn to ride by yourself."

"I'm gonna hurry."

Kelly laughed. Jace rode and rode. He

rounded the fence with precision. She loved watching him. He and the horse rode as one, each in sync with the other. Kelly thought he was truly poetry in motion. He rounded the second fence and headed for them. The sound of the horse's hooves grew louder as he came closer. Kelly remembered this sound. She knew it intimately, knew the feeling of controlling a thousand-pound animal. Jace knew it better than she did. He was masterful.

As he rode by her, she felt the wind against her face. The smell of man and horse lingered after he headed for the front fence again. Completing three more revolutions, he slowed the mare, walking her around the track until she cooled down. Then he slid to the ground in front of them.

"Dad," Ari said, wiggling through the fence. "Will you teach me to do that?"

Jace lifted him in his arms. "One day," he said. "But we have to take it slowly, okay?"

"Okay," Ari replied, smiling.

Kelly knew he didn't understand the concept of time yet. He didn't understand that it would take him years to learn to ride like

Jace did. But his enthusiasm would hold until that happened.

"Thanks," Jace said, keeping his gaze on her. "I missed doing that."

She nodded. Her heart thumped and she felt as if he was holding her, even though they were on opposite sides of the fence.

"I have a surprise for you," Kelly said. Summoning her courage, she pulled the envelope from her pocket and handed it to him.

"What's this?"

"It's where you can find your brother."

JACE STARED AT what Kelly was holding. Glancing at her, she pushed the envelope closer toward him. He took it and quickly pulled out a single sheet of paper. He read it three times. This was what he wanted. He wanted to find Sheldon and now he knew where his half brother was.

"Have you read it?" Jace asked.

Kelly nodded. "It was addressed to me."

"He wants me to contact him."

"Are you going to?"

Jace didn't immediately answer. This was something he wanted from first finding out that the Kendall had been sold. He wanted to confront Sheldon, wanted to know if there was anything they could do to retake the property. And now he had a method of doing that.

Yet, now he was hesitating. There were other factors in play that he hadn't anticipated, mainly how he felt about the woman standing before him.

"Jace?"

"I'm not sure." Jace spoke the truth. He couldn't tell her what he was going to do. He didn't know.

THE FACT THAT his half brother was alive and living in North Carolina wasn't the only interesting information Jace had found out today.

Jace paid for and collected Ari's bowl of ice cream and his own milkshake and found a booth in the back of the ice-cream shop for him and his son.

"Aren't you gonna have ice cream, Dad?" Ari asked.

Jace smiled. "Not today. I'm going to drink the milkshake." Jace preferred coffee, but the only decent cup he'd had since leaving Colombia was the one Mira made several mornings ago. Jace carried the papers he'd found earlier in the attic. He'd had them for hours, but wanted to read them in solitude and at the Kendall there was every chance Kelly could walk in on him.

Jace opened the envelope with the papers he'd found; they'd looked to be copies of the mortgage transfer documents. Kelly had told him nothing was locked. Maybe some places should be.

Jace hadn't been part of many contracts. Much of the information in them was Greek to him. He needed to make sure he followed through, though on any opportunity that presented itself. Ari deserved nothing less.

"Jason, Jason Kendall. Oh, man, it *is* you."

Both Jace and Ari looked up. A man in a dark suit and white shirt stood in front of their booth. "Douglas, Doug Thurston," he grinned, pumping Jace's hand.

"You're the last guy I expected to find here," Doug said. "Are you back or just visiting?"

"I'm here for a while," he answered. Gesturing at Ari, whose eyes were wide and staring at the new arrival, he introduced them.

"This is my son, Ari. Ari, this man is an old friend of mine."

"Hello," Doug said and offered his hand. "How old are you?"

Ari put his hand in the larger one and said, "I'm four." He emphasized the word *four* saying it louder than anything else and holding up three fingers.

"Four, you're a really big boy."

"And I help my dad all the time," he replied.

"Great. Do you hire out?"

Ari looked confused. "It was a joke, Ari," Jace said. Ari went back to his sundae.

"What are you doing here?" Jace asked Doug.

"This is still the best ice-cream store in three counties," Doug said. "I'm on my way home and thought I'd stop in and get some of that—"

"Nutty Black Cherry," they said simultaneously.

"It's still a favorite." Doug grinned.

"Sit down a moment."

Doug signaled to the clerk, then slid into the booth with Jace. "What are you doing now?" Jace asked.

"You'll never believe it, but I'm a lawyer."

Jace stared at him for a moment before bursting into laughter. "The terror of Duchess County is now an attorney?"

"Three-piece suit and all," Doug said, indicating his clothes. "I live over in York now."

"Married, children?"

"Wife of six years, baby girl, eleven months, most gorgeous child on earth."

Jace smiled. "And your practice. Are you with someone or on your own."

"I struck out on my own two years ago. Things are going well."

"Glad to hear that," Jace said and he really meant it. The two of them were lucky to have survived their reckless teenage years. The last sheriff who caught them had wised them up—thankfully—telling them their choices were to either end up dead or in jail. Jace didn't take him seriously, at first, but decided to give school a try. It would get him out of the Kendall and his father didn't care. The old man was always willing to pay for him to go away. And despite his delinquent talents, he was a good student. Doug must have gotten the message, too. They each went their own way and the sheriff's prediction remained untrue.

"So what are you doing?" Doug asked.

"I spent several years in South America, but I'm back at the Kendall. I'm helping get the place in order."

"I heard it was sold to Kelly Ashton of all people."

"Why of all people?" Jace asked.

"You don't remember her? The little kid who used to sit on the fence and watch us. She was always there, looking over the horses and wishing she could ride one."

"Sheldon probably wouldn't allow it," Jace suggested.

"It wasn't him. Your old man would holler at her every time he saw her. She'd hide among the trees. I knew she just wanted to be part of the place. She was like you, Jason. She loved the horses."

"There were no horses left at the Kendall when I arrived," Jace said. "Apparently, they were all sold before the place was."

"What a shame. It would be fun to tear through the county again on horseback." Doug chuckled. Jace knew he was reliving the past. For a second, Jace thought of riding. He could almost feel the unique exhilaration he felt for the second or two he and horse were airborne.

"There are only two mares there now. Ari and I ride them. But nothing like you and I used to."

"How long are you planning to stay at the Kendall?" Doug asked.

"I don't know."

"Dad, we're staying, right?" Each time someone mentioned them leaving, Ari was afraid it might be true.

"Yes, Ari, we're staying." His son had bonded so quickly to the Kendall. Jace knew it was the stability that the Kendall represented that appealed so strongly to Ari; he understood that staying here would mean a better life than wandering the world.

"Doug, you might just be the person I'm looking for."

"How's that?" Doug asked.

"I need a lawyer."

CHAPTER ELEVEN

SLEEPING WAS SOMETHING Jace never had a problem with. But for the past few days, he'd found it hard to slip into the familiar darkness and rest. His childhood came back. It was the letter Kelly had given him from Sheldon. Why would he write it? What could he want after all this time? The area where the letter was posted was a notoriously rich community. While Sheldon had lost the Kendall, he'd obviously landed on his feet.

Jace imagined him living high and hearty, sailing on the cruisers that dotted the bay like huge dollar signs. He wanted to feel good about his brother having taken the time to write to him. But maybe Sheldon just wanted to rub in his new wealth?

Flipping over in bed, Jace punched the pillow hard. He tried several times to find a comfortable place, but sleep was not on his agenda that night.

What should he do? Now that the opportunity was there, now that Jace knew where to contact his brother, why was he hesitating? Why didn't he respond? Why didn't he tell his brother that he never wanted to see him again? Or why didn't he tell him he wanted to know how to get the Kendall back and wanted his help?

Images of Sheldon berating him in front of his friends came back. Thoughts of him refusing any request Jace made came back. But the worst was Laura. She was his girlfriend, Jace's. Yet Sheldon was the one she chose. Jace had resolved this years ago and promised never to set foot in Windsor Heights again.

But now there was Ari. The child changed all that. Jace would do anything for his son. Even return to the Kendall. Jace knew where Sheldon was—he had to do something. He had to answer the letter. See what he wanted. Find out if he was still the conceited jerk he'd been when the two of them occupied space in this house that Kelly had restored so well.

Kicking the covers off, Jace got out of bed. There was a desk in the room, but no paper he could find. There was some in Kelly's office.

He went there and switched the light on. By the copier, he found paper with the Kendall logo on it. It must be part of the new image Kelly was making for the house and grounds.

He didn't take time to wonder if he should use it. Putting the paper on the desk, he grabbed a pen and wrote the date on the top. Then *Dear Sheldon*. After that he paused. Jace could think of nothing else to say. He had no idea what his brother wanted. He couldn't use his only reason for wanting to find Sheldon. The two weren't brothers. They couldn't depend on each other, couldn't count on each other for anything. They'd never had that kind of relationship. So why would Sheldon help him retake the Kendall?

In the end he wrote, *I'm back. I live at the Kendall. Why are you looking for me?* He signed it with only a *J*. Pulling an envelope with the new logo, he addressed it to his brother and slipped the folded paper inside.

"Jace?"

Twisting around in a swivel chair, Jace saw Kelly standing in the doorway. She wore a nightgown covered with a robe. It was white and her red hair contrasted with it starkly. During the day, she pulled her hair back. Tonight it was loose and pretty, framing her face.

"What are you doing here?" Kelly asked.

He held up the envelope he'd just sealed.

"Have you answered Sheldon?" She took a step into the room.

"If I'm going to get any sleep, I have to find out what he wants."

"He's been keeping you awake?"

"His letter," Jace said. "I can't imagine why he wants me to contact him, but I'm willing to ask. He could want to put me in my place again."

"You don't believe that?" Kelly said.

"Can you think of why he'd want to find me? We were never friends, let alone brothers. He lives in a well-to-do area, which means he's somehow got plenty of money. Why would he need to see me?"

Kelly shook her head. "I don't know, but there are other reasons."

"Give me one?"

"The olive branch," she said.

Jace made a sound that was a combination of a laugh and a grunt. "I don't think the olive branch was part of his education."

Jace's task completed, it was time to return

to bed, but Kelly standing in front of him had him wanting to wrap his arms around her. His thoughts got worse when she came to the desk and reached over him for a stamp. He could feel her warmth. She was barely an inch from him as she moved back and handed him the postage to add to the letter.

"I'll take it to the post box in the morning," she said.

Her voice felt distant as he tried to concentrate on her words, but her hair fell over her shoulder and brushed his arm as she moved. He inhaled deeply. His hand shook as he put the stamp in place. It was crooked on the top of the envelope when he finished.

THE NEXT MORNING the routine began. Jace and Ari were up at dawn and riding the fences. Ari sat in front of Jace and pretended to have control. He was too short and the horse too big for him, but Kelly remembered this was the way she'd started. She remembered her dad holding her as they rode, keeping her safe. She knew exactly what Ari was feeling.

And she envied him.

Even though Jace added his daily rides with his son to his schedule, he didn't shirk his duties. He and Ari repaired, replaced and made new the items on Kelly's list. He even added tasks that needed attention without her asking him to.

Kelly often heard the horses whinnying from the barn. The sound was like a siren's draw. She wanted to go out riding. She wanted to feel the horse under her, the gentle rhythm of its cadence. She wanted to guide it over the grounds and look at all the Kendall had and what it could be—would be.

Taking her mind off the horses, Kelly turned to go back to the books.

"Wanna go for a ride?" Jace was standing in the doorway. "How about it?"

"I'm very busy here," she said. She looked around the office. Surprisingly the room was clear of clutter and didn't seem like anyone needed to be working there.

"I saw you," he said.

"Saw me? Where?"

"In the window." He indicated the one that looked out on the back lawn.

Kelly glanced at the sunny pane.

"I saw you standing there watching us. You wanted to go for a ride. I could see it. So don't act like you're indifferent to the horses."

The color rose in her face. The word *indifferent* had been used before and from his mouth. After he'd had it on hers. Jace extended his hand. "Come on, ride with me."

"Where's Ari?"

"I've hired a baker to be on-site to prepare cookies and cakes, and other sweets for sale when the guests are here. She's showing Ari how to make cookies."

Jace offered his hand. Kelly stared at it for a long time before she covered the distance between them and put her hand in his. Within minutes they were cantering across the lawn. After a while, both of them stepped up the pace until they were galloping along the white fence where she used to sit and watch.

This was exactly as Kelly knew it would be. She felt the wind pulling her hair loose. It blew her blouse against her breasts and it billowed out the back like a sail. She raced the wind and Jace. In all these years, she hadn't forgotten how to handle a horse. She loved this feeling, the freedom of riding, of not having to worry about anything except the exhilaration of connecting with such an amazing animal.

They'd ridden a long distance from the house. The lawn had turned into a rolling landscape of lush trees. Kelly pulled the horse to a stop and got down. She tied the reins to a low branch. The animals needed to rest.

Walking to the fence, she climbed up to sit on the top rung. Jace tied his horse to the same branch and came over. He didn't climb up, but stood next to her, facing the road. Kelly would pay for this ride tomorrow. Already she could feel the unaccustomed muscles tightening. But she wouldn't mind. It was worth it just to be on a horse again.

"Is this your spot?" Jace repeated.

"My spot?" she asked.

"Your place? The one that you go to when you're alone and afraid. The place you use to think things over."

She nodded. How did he know? "I used to come here often when I lived in Short Hills."

"Why?"

"After my mother died, my father changed. He drank. A lot. I felt lost, like no one wanted me."

"How old were you when your mother died?"

Kelly let her breath out slowly. A surge of

emotion gathered in her chest and cut off her ability to speak, at first. "I was fourteen." She glanced in the direction from which they had come. "If it wasn't for the horses, I don't think I'd be here today."

"How did they help?"

It would be hard for her to explain. "They were there," she said simply.

"Did you whisper to them?"

She shook her head. "I just watched them." Kelly stared in the direction of the spot where she used to get off the school bus. She was really looking into the past. "They were huge, gorgeous, proud animals. I loved watching them. I could get lost in their movements. After a while I thought they'd miss me if I wasn't on the fence. I knew I'd miss them. So I watched them every day."

"And you found peace."

"Some measure of it." That had been so long ago. Kelly thought it could have happened to a different person. No one she knew had lost their mother. Some kids had divorced parents, but they were alive and they either knew where they were or they visited them. She felt so alone. And what was even worse was that her father went from the loving man who'd held her safe in his lap to a stranger who could only be consoled by a bottle of Kentucky Bourbon.

"Who taught you to ride?" Jace asked.

"My dad. He put me on a horse when I was five years old. After that I pestered him every day to let me ride again. Eventually, I got to ride the quarter horses and exercise some of the others."

"And you stood in for him when he was too drunk to work," Jace said.

Kelly whipped around to focus on him. "How did you know?"

"I observed a little, too."

"But he didn't work here."

"And I didn't confine my antics to this farm, either," Jace said.

"You saw me?" Kelly frowned.

"I didn't know it was you. I saw your hair." He gave her a big smile.

Suddenly self-conscious, Kelly used her hand to smooth down her hair.

She'd never noticed him glancing in her direction when she was working in place of her father. Kelly had her foot wrapped around the fence post, and her balance was off. She moved to get down.

Jace stepped back and reached over to help her. Her hands went to his shoulders and his caught her around the waist. Jace set her on the ground, but didn't release her immediately. Kelly looked up at him, her hands still on his shoulders.

"We've been here before," she said.

"Yes, we have."

"And we decided you wouldn't confuse me."

"Not we," he said. *"You."*

Jace slipped his arms around her, drawing her closer to him. His head dipped and he kissed her. She didn't try to stop him. His mouth was warm on hers and it had been a long time since someone had held her. She let herself relax and enjoy the sensation. But she had to stop this. Slowly she pushed him away.

"This is more confusing than I thought it would be." She wanted to leave, but she was pressed up against the fence. Jace must have sensed her wishes. He moved away, putting more distance between them.

"We'd better get back," he said. "I need to try Ari's cookies."

CHAPTER TWELVE

FINALLY, AFTER MONTHS OF PREPARATION, it was the day before the Kendall would be open to the public. Kelly was preoccupied with checking that everything was in order.

"Any questions?" she asked the college students who'd been hired to escort the visitors around the main house and property. One young woman raised her hand.

"What time are we to be here?"

"The tours begin at ten. Please be here by nine to get dressed in your costumes."

The woman nodded.

"For those posted along the tour, does everyone know where their station is?" She noted the nodding heads. "Is there a problem with anyone's costume? Bad fit? Items missing?" Again the nodding. "Then I'll see you tomorrow at nine."

They dispersed, returning to cars and vans parked in the lot on the opposite side of the road. Kelly ran her hands down her pants. She was nervous about the next day. So much was riding on it. Her entire future was at stake. And there was one more task she needed to do for the benefit of the Kendall's opening.

And she wasn't looking forward to it.

Kelly headed for the kitchen. She'd get a soft drink and go out to find Jace. The kitchen was hot and filled with people, all preparing for tomorrow.

"How is everything," she asked the head baker, Mrs. Templeton. They would have homemade baked goods to not only make the house smell delicious, but also for people to purchase to eat while visiting or to take with them.

Grabbing three colas from the fridge, she went out the back door. She didn't see Jace anywhere, and she didn't hear Ari's laughter. They were usually with the horses when they weren't fixing anything. Kelly headed in that direction. The barn was empty when she got there except for the two horses.

Where could they be? she wondered. Returning to the house, she looked in all the rooms, but they weren't there. Then she heard the unmistakable sound of the truck. Kelly had been so busy with the students that she hadn't realized Jace had left the property. Going to the porch, she watched Ari get out of the cabin as soon as the vehicle stopped. "Kelly! Kelly!" he called her name as he sprinted toward her.

She came down a few steps to meet him. "Not so fast, Ari."

"You should see what I got. Dad bought me a…a…" He looked to his father for further explanation.

Jace got out of the truck carrying a box from Hector's Riding Store. It was a local shop that sold boots and riding gear.

"A habit," Jace said.

"That's it," Ari went on, still as excited as a four-year-old could be. "And we got boots, too. I can't wait to ride with them. I saw this picture in the store of a boy on a horse. He looked just like me in my boots."

Kelly smiled. Ari was so exuberant. She couldn't be anything but happy around him. Jace, however, was a different story. He walked slowly to the stairs, but didn't climb them. He put a foot on the bottom step and leaned forward, looking at her.

"Ari, why don't you go to the kitchen and ask Mrs. Templeton to open this for you." She handed him one of the soft drinks.

"I can tell her about my hat…"

"Habit," Kelly corrected.

Taking the can, he ran up the stairs and into the house. Kelly could hear him calling the baker's name as he headed for the kitchen.

"I brought one for you, too," Kelly said, extending the can to him. Jace took it and moved back. She only realized she wanted him to come forward when he retreated. If he was adhering to her wishes that she not be confused by his kisses, he was already too late.

"Why were you waiting for us?" he asked. "Is there something we need to do?"

"I want you to leave," Kelly said.

Jace's eyes grew wide.

"Now?"

"Tomorrow," Kelly clarified. "The first open house is tomorrow. Everything is ready. You said you didn't…wouldn't," she corrected, "wouldn't be part of the open house. So tomorrow will you take Ari out until the event is over? It's from ten to six."

"Ari wants to be here. He's very excited about the *guests* coming. That's Ari's word. He believes it'll be a party and it'll be his first."

"You know it's not a party. Why didn't you explain it to him."

"I tried, but he still thinks that if a lot of people are coming and all those cakes are baking in the kitchen, there must be a party."

"I see he's becoming very accustomed to things around here," Kelly said with a smile.

"I thought it would be harder, but with the horses and you." Jace stopped while she processed that.

"I haven't been around small children much," she said, "but Ari is such a ball of energy. Everything is new and exciting to him."

"He loves you like a— Well, all the while we were shopping, he was insisting he had to show you his new clothes."

Kelly felt her entire body suffuse with color. "I like Ari, too."

A long moment passed between them and Kelly wondered if they were still only talking about the child. She couldn't imagine the house without Ari scampering through it.

"About tomorrow," Kelly went back to her task.

"Ari has a doctor's appointment tomorrow. He understands we'll be away for most of the day. I'm sure we can find something else to do until after six."

Jace's voice seemed to hold an angry note, but he was fighting to conceal it. Without opening the soft drink, he went up the porch steps and into the house, leaving her alone.

Kelly wasn't supposed to feel this way. She wasn't usurping his place in the Kendall. The farm belonged to her. It was her domain. And she had no choice about the open house. This was the only solution. She wished Jace would embrace it.

THE NEXT DAY arrived sunny and warm. Mrs. Templeton and her assistants were already busy in the kitchen. The smells permeating through the air were bound to make people want to purchase the cakes and cookies on offer. Kelly hadn't heard Ari or Jace that morning. She looked out the window where they often rode, but saw only empty lawn. For a split second, she wished she was with them. She wanted to go to Ari's doctor's appointment, wanted to know if he would get better.

The clock in the hall read nine-thirty. All the students were in their places. *Suppose no one comes?* The thought crossed her mind. She clenched her teeth. She'd spent so much money on this venture. The first car pulled into the lot at nine forty-five. Five people got out of it and went to the ticket booth. Kelly let out a breath. "This might work," she said to no one.

Kelly's day was filled with small accidents, things that needed to be fixed, questions that needed answering, places she needed to keep the public away from. She didn't have enough hands to cover everything.

"The china is authentic to the house," she told a woman wearing jeans and heels high enough that her back should hurt. Opening the cabinet, she took out a dinner plate and turned it over. Imprinted there was the date and name of the pattern.

"My," she said. "I'm impressed. My grandmother had this pattern and I've lost a lot of them. Would you be willing to sell any of these."

Kelly could truly use the money, but she

couldn't part with the history of the house. Smiling sweetly at the woman, she said, "I'm sorry, but they are part of the Kendall. The house wouldn't be the same without them."

The woman smiled, handed her a card and said, "If you change your mind, I'm interested."

Kelly slipped the card in a pocket, said good day and went off to the next emergency. By noon, the place was crowded, but the college students she'd hired seemed to be handling the traffic with skill. Kelly had to rush out to the ticket counter and provide more money to make change for entry fees. By one o'clock they were running low on pastries.

Kelly didn't see Jace and Ari return. She was too busy. As she came down the stairs with an armload of flyers, she stumbled at seeing Jace. His arms came out and quickly caught her.

"Where do you want these?" he asked, taking the flyers from her hands.

"Gift shop, by the exit," she said.

He left her, heading for the door with Exit written over it. Stunned for only a moment, before someone called for her attention, she wondered what had brought him back early. And where was Ari?

Jace turned and looked at her from the doorway. She silently thanked him with a smile and a nod. Surprisingly, several of the people she used to work with at the PR firm in New York, including her ex, Perry Streeter, showed up. "Your big debut! We've been anticipating this for some time now," Perry said.

"Oh, have you?" Kelly asked flatly. The small group of six were standing in the front parlor as crowds milled around them.

"Certainly," Perry said.

Kelly's frustration was growing. She had no wish to encourage Perry on any level.

"I noticed a brochure in the Maryland House as I was traveling several weeks ago," Cass Martin said. She was good at what she did. And Kelly had called her a friend while they'd worked together. But since Kelly had bought the Kendall, Cass hadn't so much as called her cell phone. "You'll have to excuse me," Kelly said. "I have a lot to do."

"No problem, we'll talk after the tour," Perry said.

"Enjoy yourselves," Kelly called as she left

them. What could they want? They didn't travel all the way from New York to see the Kendall. Did they expect her to fall on her face? And wanted to bear witness to the deed?

"Who are they?" Jace asked indicating the group from New York.

"My former colleagues from the advertising firm where I used to work."

"What do they want?"

"I haven't any idea," she said. "I'm more surprised than you that they showed up here. I can't imagine there's anything to gain."

"Maybe they're here to see you fail," Jace suggested.

Kelly's head came up quickly. She'd had the same thought.

"Don't worry. We won't let that happen." He winked at her and left to go see to whatever was needed.

We, Kelly thought. Are we a *we*?

She didn't have time to ponder that. One of the guests came up to her, a very tall statuesque woman with dark hair. She wore long pants, a short-sleeve blouse and a man's vest. On her feet were expensive leather boots. She looked every bit the horsewoman.

"You're the new owner, right?"

"Kelly Ashton." She offered her hand and the woman shook it.

"I knew your father. He'd be so proud of what you've done with the Kendall."

"I'm sorry. Your name?" Kelly asked.

"Oh, Susan Johnson. I used to work at the same farm where he worked." Susan's smile was warm and affectionate. "I was one of the people who exercised the horses. Of course, they never let me race one, but I always wanted to."

"I know what you mean," Kelly confided. "I love the feel of the wind when I ride."

"One night just as the sun was setting, your dad came to me and said one of the horses needed exercising. I thought it was strange, since I usually did this in the morning. But he led me to the track. There was a horse already there. It was Silver, a golden palomino. I'll never forget it. He told me to get in the saddle and to ride it as fast as I could all the way around the track three times."

Kelly was smiling and tears collected in the corners of her eyes.

"Do you still ride?"

"I own a horse farm in Kentucky, but when

I heard the Kendall was opening and an Ashton was responsible, I couldn't stay away."

"Thank you," Kelly said.

"No, thank you. And thanks to your father. I'll never forget him." She patted Kelly's hand, kissed her on the cheek. "I signed the guest book. You're ever in Kentucky, *please* come and see me."

She sounded sincere. "I will," Kelly told her. With a smile, she went back to her tour.

The crowd began to thin around five. Kelly was dead tired, but she was also exhilarated. She didn't know if they'd broken even according to her budget for day one, but she'd made at least five trips to the ticket counters to provide change for the entry fees. People left smiling and carrying boxes of the baked pastries to their cars.

As Kelly waved at a couple leaving, she was surprised to find her New York friends still there.

"I thought you'd gone hours ago," Kelly said, going to where they stood.

"We wanted to talk to you," Perry said.

"About what?"

He looked around. "Do you think there is a more private place we can go?"

"My office," Kelly said. It was clean and clear of any debris. She wanted them to know that she had a neat mind and a neat office, even though six people would make it crowded.

Cass closed the door after the last of them came inside.

"I apologize for the space. I rarely have more than a couple of people in here at a time." She rarely had anyone in there. Jace had come and Ari. The modeling agency sent a crew, but they wanted to walk the property and scout locations. Mainly the place was her sanctuary.

"All right," Kelly began. "Let's have it."

"What?" Perry asked.

"What's the real reason you're here. This is an awfully long way from Madison Avenue. And you six didn't make this trip to look at an old house."

"You've done wonders with it," Cass complimented. "From what I hear the place was a relic and you've brought it back to life."

"And I love the costumes," Alex Wheatly said. Alex had been her friend, giving her advice and keeping her abreast of the office gossip. It was Alex who informed her of Perry Streeter's promotion over her. And it was Alex who let her know that the account she'd been working on was leaving the agency.

"So you like what I've done with the place," she said, trying not to allow the sarcasm she felt to filter into her voice.

"We like the marketing ideas you used to get this place up and running," Cass said.

"They were nothing short of brilliant," Perry added.

"Thank you," Kelly said. *There has to be a shoe ready to drop,* she reminded herself. Kelly looked at them, allowing her gaze to settle on each face before she responded.

"The truth is, Kelly, we want you to come back to your old job," Perry said.

Kelly was stunned. "Return?"

"You've done a great job here. This will undoubtedly be an ongoing concern for some time," Cass explained. "But don't you miss the drumbeat of New York? You were right there with the best, coming up with the ideas, working with the staff."

Cass handled a lot of the advertising at the firm.

"Everyone liked you," Alex said.

"But according to you—" Kelly looked directly at Perry "—I lost the Grissom account. As I remember it, something in the neighborhood of six million dollars."

"Grissom is back," Alex interjected. "And they want you."

"Me, why?"

"When they left us, they didn't know what they were doing. We, and by that I mean you, gave them more customer service and better ideas than anyone else. So they want to work with us—you—again."

Kelly grinned. She understood. There was a six-million-dollar contract with a provisional clause in it.

"I'm sorry," Kelly began. "I have other obligations."

"Where?" Cass asked. "Here?"

"Yes," Kelly said, her brows rising. "Here."

"You've done an amazing job, but to handle the Grissom account…" Cass left the sentence hanging as if there was no contest between what she'd spent the past two years doing and what they were offering.

"We're prepared to double your salary," Perry said. "Think of it, twice what you made before, corner office, expense account. You can move into a swanky apartment in Manhattan and live the good life."

"You're assuming I don't have a good life here."

"Let's not rush into anything," Perry said. "Take some time to look over the offer, get used to the idea," Perry said. He pulled an envelope from his pocket and laid it on her desk. "As added incentive that loft you wanted to renovate in Soho is available. With the added salary you'd be able to afford it."

"I'll give that some consideration," Kelly said.

"Take a couple of weeks," Perry said. "I'll give you a call then and we can work out the details."

She watched as the entourage left her office and subsequently the property. Alex hung back and gave her a hug.

"I'd love to work with you again," he said.

"We were good together," she agreed. She'd enjoyed working with Alex. As the artistic director, he complemented her ideas and transformed them into visual beauty.

Admittedly Kelly was glad to see them go. Their offer was flattering, but she'd worked herself silly, put every penny she had to get this operation running. No way was she giving it up now for a loft in Soho.

With her former colleagues gone, the parking lot was empty. Kelly left her office to collect the receipts of the day. She had to pay the staff and make sure they would show up next week. Their checks were already written and in envelopes. They'd gathered in the large ballroom. Jace and Ari were there when she went in.

"Great day," one of the women said. "I had a very good time."

"Does that mean you're willing to come back next week and do it again?" Kelly asked with a smile.

"Absolutely," she said.

Kelly passed out their paychecks and said she'd expect them next week. "If anyone can't make it, please let me know as early as possible, so I can find a replacement."

"Will do," someone said.

They filed out, leaving Jace and Ari as the only people in the room with her.

"You look tired," Jace said.

"I'm exhausted," she confided. "But my day is not done. I have to count receipts."

"Want some help?" Ari piped up.

Tension drained out of her at the small child's willingness to take some of the weight off her shoulders. Dropping down to his level, she hugged him. "Thank you, but you'd better eat your dinner." She ruffled his hair. "That is if you didn't eat too many of those cakes."

"I didn't. Dad wouldn't let me." Ari twisted around to check his dad's compliance.

Kelly glanced at Jace. She stood up. "Thank you for coming back and helping. I know you didn't want to."

"You were spread too thin," Jace said.

She realized his comment wasn't censure on her decision about the house. She was glad because she was too tired for a debate.

"I have to go back to the office, but before I go what did the doctor say?"

"I don't have asama," Ari stated proudly.

"Asthma," Jace corrected. "They have to get some test results back, but he doesn't believe Ari has asthma."

"What?" A smile spread across her face. "How?"

"The doctor said he may have been allergic to something in Colombia that caused restricted air flow."

"Do they know what it was?"

Jace shook his head. "Whatever it was, we didn't bring it with us. And apparently, it's not here."

"That's why I breathe," Ari said.

"I was concerned when I bought the horses that he wouldn't be able to ride, but he's taken to them."

"What about his leg?"

Ari skipped around the room. "All gone," he said, then ran back to Jace.

"Lack of activity. And he has a shorter tendon in one leg. With exercise and time, it'll be unnoticeable."

"He does appear to have less of a limp now than he did a couple of months ago."

Jace nodded, putting his hands on Ari's shoulders.

Kelly studied the tiny face. "You're going to be fine," she told him, still smiling. Ari left his dad and ran to her. She bent down and caught the small bundle. "Congratulations. This is the best news I've had today."

"Me, too," he said. "Best news."

"You'd better go in to dinner. I'll be in as soon as I finish the receipts."

"You're exhausted," Jace said. "Why don't

you come to dinner first and then check the receipts."

"I'll be right there," she said. "I need to find out if I'm going to meet the bills this month."

CHAPTER THIRTEEN

JACE LOOKED AT his watch. Kelly hadn't come to dinner before he and Ari had finished and cleaned up. Ari practically fell asleep at the dinner table. The doctor's office and the excitement of a long day took its toll on him. It had been long for Jace, too. He went to the kitchen and made Kelly a sandwich and poured a glass of milk. Carrying the tray to her office, he went inside. She was asleep at her desk.

He hated to wake her. From the way he'd seen her rushing about, she'd had to be dead on her feet. He couldn't allow her to stay like that. It was uncomfortable and, besides, she could possibly fall. Jace put the tray on the table. Turning her chair and holding her, he lifted her into his arms with the greatest care. She stirred, but didn't come fully awake.

He refused to look at her sleeping face, but he couldn't stop her pretty scent. She used some kind of floral shampoo and the sweet smell filled his nostrils. Her skin was silky smooth and warm to his touch. Jace carefully carried her up the stairs. Gently, he laid her on the bed. He removed her shoes and pulled a spread over her. Then, taking one last look, he left the room, closing the door softly behind him.

Jace knew she worked hard to make the Kendall a going concern. And she was starting from scratch. He'd heard some of the comments today from people who knew the Kendall. They spoke of its transformation. Of what Kelly had done over the past two years to make this the showplace of the county. She had done it proud, according to one of the locals.

She'd even had the people from her former job come to visit. Jace wondered what their purpose was here. What had they discussed while cloistered in her office? And what would happen now? There was a major complication Kelly didn't know about. Yes, he'd taken Ari to the doctor this morning. But after that appointment, he'd spoken with Doug Thurston, who'd given Jace the news he wanted to hear. There was a loophole in the contract of sale.

Jace could get his home back.

THE LETTER SAT on the dresser. It had been there for three days. Sheldon hadn't mentioned it to Audrey. The return address was the Kendall and it was in Jason's handwriting. Sheldon could hardly believe it. How could Jason be living there? Sheldon was too afraid to read the letter. Strange because he'd never been afraid of anything his brother once said or did.

But now he understood Jason. In many ways, he walked in his brother's shoes and they hurt. He knew what it was to be looked down on.

He was curious to know what Jason had to say, though. The Kendall logo on the envelope was different, but it was definitely the Kendall. Had Jason found some way to…what? He couldn't own the place. Sheldon knew it was sold to a woman. Had she and Jason somehow gotten together? Many women in Windsor Heights were interested in Jason. Laura had told him. Jason was good-looking and had that strong image of the bad boy. Women loved that, she'd said. It made the guy more virile in their eyes. And women loved the challenge of taming all that strength. Well, some women.

Sheldon could possibly find all the answers to these questions if he'd just open the envelope. He would, he told himself. But not today.

Leaving the letter on the dresser, he headed out to work. He'd continue scraping hulls. Soon he would have to tell Audrey about Jason's letter. She would find a way to ask if he'd heard anything if he didn't volunteer the information.

Sheldon smiled. He liked Audrey. She was real. He could tell the difference now. Laura had been real, too. But he and Laura had lived in a different world. A world that isolated them and distorted how they should treat other people. Meanwhile, Audrey had had few privileges and when her daughter died, she took in her grandson and she was doing everything she could to fill in as a parent. But what struck Sheldon most about them is they appeared happy. They truly loved and respected each other, he thought. That's what made all the difference. That and sacrifice.

When Jason had come to stay at the Kendall after his mother died, they looked on him as a burden. How could they have been so cruel?

And how could he ever do or say anything to make up for his past actions? Maybe sending that letter had been a mistake. And the reply could be just as much a slap in the face as he deserved.

THE DOORBELL RANG as Kelly was headed to the kitchen for a second cup of coffee. She tried to limit herself to two cups a day, but in the past month she found herself wearing a path in the hall leading to the caffeine station.

Glancing at the grandfather clock sitting near the staircase, she reversed direction and went to the door. She wondered who could be seeking her out at this time. Through the heavy glass, Kelly saw the figure of a man. She opened the door to find Perry Streeter standing there. "I figured if I came in person you couldn't refuse."

"I don't understand. What are you doing here?"

He was impeccably dressed. Even though the temperature in Maryland was several degrees higher than it was in New York, Perry would never allow a drop of sweat to stain his wardrobe or his personality. He was in control, managing everything, refusing to let anyone think he wasn't the master of his fate.

Kelly knew it was a facade. He'd spent a lifetime hiding behind it. So she didn't understand why he wanted to see her. She had X-ray vision where he was concerned. And he knew it.

"Aren't you going to invite me in. I hear they do that in the South."

Kelly stood back. "Of course, come in."

She led him to her office. Just as she went through the door, she saw Jace enter the hall. Perry closed the door and turned to her.

"Why are you here?" she asked for the second time.

"No ulterior motive. I wanted to see you. It's nearly lunchtime. I thought you'd go out with me."

"Why?"

"You have to eat."

"I mean why would I go anywhere with you? There's nothing for you to gain by being with me. You told me that."

He winched at her words. "I was wrong. Why don't we run out to a local restaurant and have something to eat. You can spare an hour or two for an old friend, can't you?"

He wasn't a friend. That had ended when he told her he wanted to end their relationship, that he had found someone else.

Still, Kelly wanted to know his real reason for coming to see her and she wanted to hear about the agency. What was going on there now? She still had friends at the firm. She'd neglected them in the past few months due to the overwhelming changes she'd been working on at the Kendall.

And there was Jace. He'd taken up a lot of her thoughts.

"We don't have New York–style restaurants here. The food is simple and good."

He spread his hands as if accepting his fate.

Kelly grabbed her purse and they went back to the front door. Outside, in the circular driveway gleamed a Mercedes sports car, a two-seater, fire-engine red. It looked like Perry could have driven it off the showroom floor only moments ago.

He opened the door and helped her inside. The interior was plush with all the bells and whistles deserving of a mover and shaker in the advertising business.

"New?" she asked.

"Had it a month." He accelerated around the circle and sped down the driveway toward the road.

Kelly directed him to the diner on the main street. It was the kind of place where you seat yourself. The tablecloths were white and covered with a solid piece of clear glass. In the center was a bud vase with a plastic flower in it. The menus were already on the table, being held up by the condiments collection. Perry led her to a table next to a big window. Outside sat his car. Kelly wondered if he trusted the citizens of Windsor Heights not to dent his doors.

She lifted the menu, although she knew what she was going to have.

"What's good here?"

"Everything," she said. She looked directly at him. "I can recommend the fried chicken. I know you don't usually eat anything fried, but it's to die for. Barring that, the liver and onions are good.

"I hate liver," he said. "Do they have any fish?"

"This is Maryland," Kelly said. "The crab cakes are excellent. They alone are reason enough to drive this far."

Perry frowned.

"There's the meatloaf. It's not only good, it'll sustain you for your trip back to New York. Or are you planning to visit the area?"

"I came only to see *you*. I'll be leaving right after lunch."

Kelly's eyes opened wider.

"Why are you looking like that?" he asked.

"We've already said our last words. I find it surprising that you came all the way here to have lunch with me. You must want something. What is it?"

"I promise I only wanted to see you."

The waitress came over and Kelly ordered the cheeseburger plate. Perry opted for the Maryland Crab Cakes.

"This is a surprising turn," Perry said after the waitress left them.

"What do you mean?"

"I thought you lived on salads and bottled water."

"I get more exercise here. I still love salads and water, but I get to have all my favorites now, too."

"You really like living here?" Perry sounded as if he couldn't fathom a person preferring the quiet farm life compared to the fast-paced, nonstop existence of a throbbing city.

"You don't think there's much going on out here, right?"

He glanced around. The restaurant had several tables with people at them. Most were dressed as if they worked on farms.

"Is there?"

"This is horse country," she defended.

The waitress returned and set their plates in front of them. She smiled and left.

"Service is fast," Perry said.

Kelly knew he was thinking the food couldn't be good if it didn't take a long period of time to prepare. Her plate held a thick cheeseburger that was high with lettuce, tomato and fried onions. The rest of the plate was covered with curly French fries. Kelly dug into it as if she hadn't had anything to eat in years. Perry took a tentative bite of his crab cakes. Kelly watched him close his eyes and savor the deliciousness of the food.

"Like them?" she asked.

"They're wonderful. Who would have thought food like this would come out of a place like this."

"Careful, Perry. Your snobbery is showing."

"Sorry, I didn't mean that the way it sounded."

Kelly let his apology go. She was more interested in what else he surely wanted to say.

"Okay, Perry, I have my food now. I want to know what you want." He started to speak, but Kelly interrupted him. "Don't say you only came for lunch, because we both know you'd rather go to a four-star restaurant where people recognize you, than be in a homespun town where horseflesh is the stock in trade."

He set his fork down and folded his arms in front of him. Kelly hated this gesture. He was either gathering courage to dictate something or buying time. To her it seemed cowardly.

"I want you to give up this farm business and come back to work."

"I already have a job," she told him.

"You can't want to continue here. You're too good. And what happens when you finish the place? There'll be no job waiting for you. You'll fail."

"Fail," she said. "You think I'm going to fail?"

"Of course not. I think you'd be so much better at what you do best."

"Perry, you have no comparison for what I do best. How do you know my work at the Kendall isn't better than me selling toothpaste or cupcakes or the newest shade of lipstick?"

"Because I know you."

"Even if that's true, I get more satisfaction from working at the Kendall than I ever got working on the Crawford or Grissom accounts." The Crawford account brought in ten million dollars. It was her job to get consumers to buy their food products, specifically peanut butter and a variety of canned goods.

"What about us?" he asked.

Kelly nearly dropped her cheeseburger. "What us?"

"You know we were the best team at the agency."

Kelly understood what was happening. They weren't a team. Perry was a user. He'd used her, but she had been too blind to see what he was doing until he'd dumped her. He'd thought he could do it on his own, and when the time came for him to produce something new that the client would like, he couldn't do it. And that's why he was trying to get Kelly to change her mind.

"I have my own team here," she said. "We work well together and we get the job done."

"But think about it, Kelly. We were phenomenal. Between the two of us together, we could open our own agency."

"Perry, you don't seem to understand that I'm happy here."

He looked out the window. Kelly glanced out, too. Jace drove into the lot and parked next to the red sports car. She watched as he slid out of the cab and headed for the front door. What now? She couldn't see Jace and Perry becoming fast friends.

"If you come back, you can have your own team. It would be so much easier for you and you wouldn't have to handle every detail yourself," Perry said.

"I don't *handle* every detail here," she said. "All changes require my approval, but I don't have do them myself. I *like* doing them. If I don't do it or can't, I hire someone."

"What about that guy?"

"What guy?"

"The one who's shown up out of the blue."

The door opened and Jace walked in. "You

mean that guy?" She indicated Jace. "He's helped me out a lot and he's a friend. Now you can return to New York and put your own team together. Thanks for lunch, but I see I have a ride back to the farm." She intentionally used the word *farm*.

"I'll give you a call in a few days. Think it over. It's a good offer."

Kelly didn't need to think about his offer.

"Is everything all right here," Jace asked as he came to the table where the two of them sat.

"Yes," Kelly said. "Everything is fine." She got up and looked at Perry. "Thank you for lunch. Have a good trip back to the city." Then she looked at Jace. "Do you think I can hitch a ride back to the Kendall?"

JACE OPENED THE cab door and helped her inside. Fastening her seat belt she wondered why he'd come to find her.

"What was that all about?" Jace asked. They were on the highway, heading to the house when he spoke.

"He asked me to return to New York."

"Why?"

"I'm not really sure. I have the impression

they got some new accounts and need people who can step in and work immediately."

"I get the impression that work had nothing to do with what he wants," Jace said.

Kelly winced. She had gotten the same impression.

"You two were more than colleagues, right?"

She waited a long moment before answering. "Yes. We worked together and we were a couple. I thought we believed in the same things, wanted the same things."

"But…" he prompted.

"But he apparently he had other ideas," she said.

Jace reached the Kendall's circular drive and stopped the truck. Neither of them got out.

"What happened?" he asked.

Kelly released her seat belt and shifted in the spot to look at him. He leaned over the steering wheel, giving her his full attention.

"Working in the kind of New York agency that I did is a twenty-four hour a day job. In advertising the client always wants something new, something that will skyrocket their product to the top of the market share pyramid. And they wanted it a week ago. If that doesn't happen and the client jumps ship, the project executive and staff are usually fired."

"Is that what happened to you?" Jace asked. His voice was low and tender.

"Sort of. We were good. Perry and I came up with client after client. And they were satisfied for the most part."

"Which part *weren't* they happy with?"

"It wasn't anything monumental. One of our clients didn't like a strategy that we put in place. The product didn't sell at the expected levels they wanted."

"So they pulled up stakes?"

She nodded.

"And you got canned?"

"No, I'd already decided to leave. But Perry put the blame on me. He got the promotion that should have been mine."

"So why does he want you to come back?"

"According to some of my friends who still work there, his idea factory has dried up."

"You were the one with all the innovative ideas. And he took credit for them?"

"That sounds a little egotistical," she said, frowning.

"But it's true, right?"

"Mainly. Perry had some good ideas, but clients want great. They want buzz. They want…"

"Let me help you out here. Even for a guy who spent a lot of time in foreign countries and rarely worked inside an office, Perry or anyone for that matter is only as good as those supporting them and Perry's running scared. He's afraid the powers that be will discover that he really wasn't the driving force behind the campaigns he worked on with you. And now that you're not there his work is not as good."

"That's not totally true."

"Kelly, I've seen the changes you've made here at the Kendall. You have a good eye for both detail and the big picture. You can imagine what a room will look like before it's changed. Your ideas for marketing have changed the Kendall from a has-been to a place that people stand in line to get into. I'll bet from what you told me about the racetrack, that you already know exactly what it will look like down to the last electrical socket and light switch. You're amazing."

Pleasure washed over her. She hadn't been

complimented for her efforts by him and she was proud that he'd seen her efforts as valuable.

"Well, I don't have to worry about Perry anymore."

She opened the door and got out of the truck. The air seemed just as tense as it was inside the cab. Kelly looked up at the gleaming white house. Jace joined her.

"I have the Kendall." She turned to face him. "And the last electrical socket and light switch are in the Tidal Box, third level up, far wall, next to the private elevator."

As SOON As Jace entered Doug's office his receptionist sent him straight in. Doug stood and they shook hands.

"You've confirmed what you told me the other day?" Jace asked, getting right to the point.

"Yes. It's a technicality, but a big one. Given the number of people who read these contracts before they were signed, someone should have brought this error to light."

"Error?" Jace frowned.

"I'm sure it was, but it's binding."

"What is it?" Jace was getting antsy. He

wanted to know the details of any chance he had to take possession of the Kendall. Although, of late, watching Kelly, seeing the amount of effort she put into the place was piquing his conscience. He didn't want to hurt her.

"Usually a contract in this state gives the signers three months to rescind it, back out of it. In other words they can change their minds without any consequences. It's called a Buyer's Remorse Clause."

Jace nodded. He was aware of this rule.

"In this contract—" Doug turned the paperwork around and handed it across the desk to Jace "—it says three years, not three months. To tell you the truth, I didn't see it the first time, either. I'm so used to seeing three *months* that I read what I expected to see."

Jace looked down at the papers. The words *three years* had been underlined in red.

"As Ms. Ashton has only owned the house for two years, you can challenge the contract—the sale."

Jace looked up. Kelly's face, framed with her brilliant red hair, flashed before his eyes. She'd worked so hard in the past two years.

And she was only seeing the value of that now. An image of her running around, taking care of the details of the open house assaulted him as clearly as if he'd been hit.

"It would be a long road," Doug said.

Jace focused on him. "How so?"

"You'd have to pay whatever the outstanding taxes were, which would be substantial at this point. After that you'd have to invoke your father's will."

"Challenge the will?" Jace said.

"By arguing that you should have inherited it in the first place."

"My father didn't recognize me in the will. He left the property solely to my brother Sheldon."

"Where is Sheldon?"

Jace shrugged. "He's in North Carolina."

"Have you had any contact with him in the past two years?"

"Only just recently, but we were never really friends even though we were half brothers."

Doug leaned back in his chair and whistled. "This whole business could bankrupt you and in the end you might still lose." He paused, letting Jace take it all in. Then he asked. "What do you want to do?"

Jace stared at the papers, the red underlining reminding him of the bloodline he expected to secure for Ari. When he looked up, Doug was staring intently at him.

"Let me think about it for a few days. I'll get back to you."

Jace left the lawyer's office then. He tucked the contract in his pocket, but didn't go to the truck and start for the Kendall. He walked. He needed time to think about things. He was growing closer and closer to Kelly. She'd taken him and his son in when they showed up out of the blue, and she gave him a job. In essence, she provided him with the insurance Ari needed and a place for him to grow and thrive. Now Jace was going behind her back and trying to take away what she'd worked so hard for.

But it should have been his. Or at least partly his. *He* should have the right to pass it on to his son. How had things gotten so out of control? Jace needed to talk to Sheldon. Jace had to make some decisions about Ari, about their future. If he decided to fight for the Kendall, it would be expensive and take a lot of time. During the process, he'd need somewhere else to stay. He'd have to uproot Ari again and the child was just getting used to being with Kelly and the horses. Ari loved the horses. Removing him would hurt.

If he didn't pursue the Kendall, they still needed someplace to live. They couldn't go on staying at the Kendall and having Kelly support them. Turning around, Jace returned to the truck and headed for the farm. He'd begun to think of it as home, but the Kendall had never been his home. As much as he wanted it to be. As much as he wanted all the love due a son and a brother, he never got it and he would never be able to give it to his own son.

They were going to have to make other arrangements. Being at the Kendall had been a mistake. Getting to know Kelly had been a mistake, too.

CHAPTER FOURTEEN

THE MAIN HOUSE WAS empty when Jace returned. There were no smells coming from the kitchen. No sounds of movement anywhere. Shrugging out of his jacket, he hung it on the coat tree and called, "Ari?" No answer. "Kelly?" No answer.

After a moment, he went to her office. The room was neat, but empty. He looked out of the window at the horse barn. There was no sign of them anywhere. The kitchen looked as if they'd just up and left. The coffeemaker was off, but it had a timer that would turn it off after an hour, so they could have been gone that long or longer. The remnants of breakfast, however, still lay on the table. Discarded eggs and toast had dried on the plate. Coffee in the cups was cold. Even Ari's bowl of cereal was soggy and abandoned.

"What happened?" he muttered, fear invading his heart.

Then he heard car doors and people talking loudly. Quickly, he headed for the front door. Ari was the first to see him.

"Dad," he called. "Kelly's hurt."

Jace was down the steps before his son had finished speaking. He ran to Mira and Drew's truck. Kelly was in the backseat. Mira was driving. Jace yanked the door open and looked at her.

"She's all right," Ari said, standing next to him. "We went to the hospital."

"I'm fine," Kelly told them.

"She's not fine," Mira warned, also standing next to him. "She fell off the horse and it kicked her."

Jace's eyes opened wide. "They're very gentle horses," he said. "I would never bring unsettled horses here unless we were ready for them."

"Let's just get her inside," Mira said. "We'll explain there."

Jace reached for Kelly, lifting the pale red-head into his arms. He carried her into the house and upstairs to her room, Mira and Ari on his heels.

"How did this happen?" Jace asked, after

Kelly was in bed and Mira had pulled the covers over her.

"Later," she whispered.

"Kelly?" Ari stood beside her and spoke in a low voice. "Are you gonna be okay?"

Kelly gave him a weak smile. "Yes," she said. "I'll be good as new in the morning." She was drowsy, her eyelids closing heavily.

"The doctor gave her pain medication. She'll be asleep in a moment," Mira told him.

Ari slipped his hand in Jace's and looked up at him. "Is she really okay?"

Jace lifted the child into his arms. "She'll be fine."

"Let's let her sleep," Mira said.

Jace backed out of the room. Mira followed, closing the door.

"Is her leg sprained?" Jace asked. It had been thickly bandaged.

Mira nodded.

"But she's always so active. And there's a lot going on." Jace should have been here. While he was off looking for a way to get the Kendall back, she was falling off a horse, one that he had brought to the farm. He felt responsible.

Ari loved Kelly. He'd taken to her almost

from the first. Jace realized his son wasn't just having medical issues. Those had cures or controls, whereas missing a mother was something entirely different.

He wasn't sure he knew what to do about it. His feelings for Kelly were definitely there, but if he pursued the lawsuit for Ari's sake as much as his own, he'd cause her pain. Worse.

She'd never forgive him.

KELLY MOANED AS she woke up. Her head ached and any movement made it worse. She opened her eyes. Jace smiled at her. He was sitting on the side of the bed. She was glad to see him. Even with the headache, she felt a little better knowing he was there and that he'd been close by.

"How long have you been sitting there?" she asked.

"Not long," he said. "How do you feel?"

"Like I've been kicked by a horse."

He smiled. "You can joke, so you must be feeling better."

"Where's Ari?"

"In the kitchen with Mira."

"She's still here?"

"She wouldn't leave until she knew you were all right."

"How's Ari?" she asked.

Jace frowned. "Why Ari? Was he hurt by the horse?"

"No," she tried to shake her head, but the pain was too much.

"I have a headache," Kelly said.

"You'll feel better after you eat something."

"I *am* hungry," she said.

"Good, that's a positive sign."

"Is this your own diagnosis, doctor?" She tried to joke, but Jace looked really concerned. Kelly wondered if Mira had told him what happened.

"It is."

"Don't worry. The doctor said I'd be fine in a few days."

"Mira said you fell off one of the horses."

"Clumsy of me." She smiled, even though the effort caused pain.

"I'll go and get you something to eat," Jace offered. He got up, allowing Kelly to move her legs toward the side of the bed.

"I'm sure I can eat in the kitchen." She

started to sit up. Pain gripped her. She fought through it and put her feet on the floor.

Jace eased her back into the bed. "No need. How often do you get breakfast in bed? Take advantage of it."

Kelly was glad to lay back down. She didn't want to move for decades or at least until her headache was relieved. Her leg felt tight, but better than her head. She wanted to see it, see if there was a bruise or any broken skin. After the horse kicked her, she'd grabbed for her leg. The severe pain had caused tears to flow from her eyes. Mira came running and after one look, she was on the phone, calling for help.

The doctors told her she was very lucky. Kelly knew it. She'd seen accidents with horses before and she was usually very careful. But when she saw Ari running toward her, his innocent body unaware of the danger, she miscalculated and tried to get down when she was in the process of getting in the saddle. Her foot caught and she scared the mare. It naturally balked and kicked out, clipping her on the ankle.

Ari had cried on the way to the hospital and his face was still damp when they'd wheeled her into the waiting room and pronounced her well enough to go home. He'd dried his eyes only when she hugged him and assured him she was all right.

Kelly pushed the covers back. She rolled onto her side and with effort sat up. She was still wearing her clothes, although one pant leg had been cut for the doctors. Carefully, she pushed the torn pant leg aside.

"Oh," she gasped, seeing the black-and-blue marks on an ankle the size of a grapefruit.

"What are you doing?" Jace came in. Quickly, he set her tray on a table and rushed to her, lifting her back in the bed.

"According to Mira, the doctor said you need to stay immobile for at least twenty-four hours or until the swelling goes down."

Kelly fell back against the pillows, feeling completely defeated.

"Can I see Ari?" she asked.

"Sure, he's clamoring to see if you're all right."

Kelly smiled with effort. Jace retrieved her tray. He sat it in front of her and handed her two pain pills.

Taking the glass of orange juice from the

tray, she swallowed the medication and drank the entire contents of the glass.

"I know what Mira said, but I think you'd better tell me what happened." Jace sat in the chair next to the bed.

She told him the whole story as well as she could remember it. "You didn't say anything to Ari?" she asked, concerned for the boy.

"No," he said.

"It wasn't his fault. He didn't know he could spook the horse. I should have..."

Jace leaned over and brushed his lips over hers. Kelly's eyes opened wide.

"I understand," he said. "But he needs to know how to properly work around animals."

"Kelly, Kelly," Ari shouted as he ran down the hall. Kelly heard him coming. Jace moved away from her and as the little ball of energy came into the room and headed directly for the bed, Jace caught him before he launched himself onto the spread and upset Kelly and her breakfast tray.

"Good morning." Kelly smiled at him, hoping the pain didn't show on her face.

"You slept a really long time," he said. He looked at his dad. "Dad said we needed to be quiet. I was quiet."

"I didn't hear you at all," she told him.

"Is your leg better?"

"It's swollen, but that will go down soon."

"Can you walk? Dad carried you up here."

She remembered. Even in the haze of medication, Jace holding her had been familiar. Kelly thought about the night of the open house. She remembered being in her office, putting the receipts in the safe and looking at her computer. The next thing she knew it was morning and she was fully dressed, in her bed, with the spread over her. She had no recollection of how she got there, but some dreamlike memory felt the strong arms that carried her.

"Ari, we need to let Kelly rest now," Jace said.

"She rested all night." Ari's logic tickled her. "Didn't you, Kelly?"

"You're right, Ari. I did rest all night, but the medicine makes me sleepy."

"Okay. When it's lunchtime, are you going to eat in bed?"

"I have to keep my foot up, so I might have to stay here," Kelly explained.

"Can I eat in bed with you?" he asked.

"Maybe."

"Wow!" he said. "What about tomorrow? Will we eat in bed then, too?"

"Tomorrow I might be able to eat at the table if your dad will help me get there."

Ari turned around sharply to look at Jace. "You will, won't you, Dad?"

Jace bent down to Ari and said, "I will if you promise me something?"

"What?"

"Promise me that you won't go running after the horses even if you see me or Kelly getting on them. You'll always, always call us first. So you won't get hurt?"

Ari had given his full attention to Jace when his voice became serious.

"I promise," he said. Then he looked at Kelly. "Did I hurt you?"

"No," she and Jace said at the same time.

"The horse hurt me, Ari," Kelly said. "I need to be careful, too. And I wasn't. That's why I got hurt."

"You'll be careful, too?"

"I will," she told him. "I promise."

"We have to go now, Ari." Jace caught the boy's hand.

"Ari?" Kelly called. He faced her. "Do you think I could have a hug?"

He smiled and ran to the bed, reached up and Kelly leaned down and hugged him.

He let go and turned to his dad. "You hug her, too, Dad."

Kelly felt the color drain from her face. Then a flash fire took possession of her and her face was no less red than a cooked lobster. Glancing at Jace, she saw his face reflecting the exact same color.

KELLY'S LEG WAS still throbbing when she woke for lunch four hours later. The swelling had gone down some, but not totally. Mira came up and helped her wash and change clothes. The effort took more energy than she thought it would.

"Where's Ari and Jace?" Kelly asked.

"In the kitchen. Ari is making you a special lunch. At least, he's trying to, and Jace…" She seemed to intentionally leave the sentence hanging.

"What about him?"

"You're attracted to him." Mira stated it as if the entire world knew it to be true.

Kelly didn't bother to deny it. "Nothing new, I'm afraid. You know I've been drawn to him since he was a wild teen riding across the fields."

"But this time, he's attracted to you, too."

Kelly leaned on the cane she'd come home from the hospital with and stared at her cousin.

"Don't look at me like that. You should see how *he* looks at *you* when you're not paying attention."

"That's just because of Ari," Kelly said.

"It's not only because of Ari. When he carried you out of the truck yesterday, he held you as if you were the most precious thing on earth."

"I'm sure you're wrong. I'm betting Jace wants the Kendall. He's only hanging around here until he can get on his feet and find a permanent place." Kelly said the words, but she knew the man who'd kissed her, and those kisses couldn't be delivered by someone who had no feelings for her.

"If you say so."

Kelly knew Mira didn't believe her. She didn't truly believe her own words.

"I can have proof in just a moment. He's coming up to carry you downstairs," Mira said. The smirk on her face was unmistakable.

As it was, both Kendall males came to fetch her. Jace didn't hesitate. He swept her into his arms and carried her down the stairs and into the large kitchen. The table was set for five and everyone took a seat. Drew arrived just as they were sitting. Since Mira had come to help for a few days, Drew had joined her.

Kelly glanced at Jace. She considered whether Mira saw something she had not. Sure he'd kissed her more than once and she enjoyed it. She admitted she wouldn't mind exploring where their relationship might go, but she still had a purpose that took top priority in her life. Men, she knew, could complicate that. Did Jace?

His coming to the Kendall had nothing to do with her. Even when they were kids, he had never really looked at her. She had noticed him, though. Often she could only see him from a distance. Yet secretly she wanted him to notice her, too. But he was into himself, his problems, and his efforts to get his father's attention. From what Kelly could tell, that never happened. She didn't know that at the time. She thought he was rebelling, like most teenagers. And then he was gone. For months she wouldn't see him. Then she'd get off the bus to watch the horses and he'd be racing along the far fence or driving through town as fast as the car would go.

But even her red hair, which everyone said was like watching fire burn, wasn't bright enough for him to see her. She was invisible perched on that fence.

"You're very quiet," Jace said. "Are you in pain?"

Kelly shook her head. "My leg is beginning to tingle."

"Wow. Tingle," Ari said. "Tingle, tingle, tingle."

He must have liked the sound of the word, since he repeated it several more times.

"What do you mean?" Jace asked.

Kelly could feel the vibes coming from Mira. She refused to look at her cousin for fear she'd say or do something to give Kelly away. "The doctor said that was a sign it was healing."

"Put no weight on it for three full days," Jace said.

She nodded.

"He just wants to carry you around," Mira said teasingly.

"I do," Jace admitted. "It's the hair." He indicated Kelly's red hair. "It smells good."

Mira laughed. "It used to smell like horses."

"I've grown up," Kelly said. "Now I wash it."

"Can I wash it?" Ari asked.

Kelly suddenly had an image of Ari's little hands tangling in her mass of hair.

She hadn't said anything and the child must have thought she was going to say no. As a suggestion, Ari said, "Dad can help."

Mira and Drew laughed. Kelly and Jace turned red.

KELLY HADN'T BEEN in her office in days and she was glad to be ambulatory again, even if it was with a cane. The swelling had gone down on her ankle enough for her to put on shoes. She finally had a chance to feel elated at the income from the first open house. They'd taken in enough fees to cover the expenses for the month. The next four weeks would be gravy. Kelly looked up from her computer screen. Tears gathered in her eyes and rolled down her cheeks. It worked, she thought. She was going to be able to support the house at least through the summer and fall seasons. Winter would have far fewer visitors. She'd been working on school programs, but they required deep discounts to look appealing. Still…

More than likely, there would be some loss leaders, but over time they would gain other paying guests.

She went back to the computer. She needed to prepare for the next open house. Even though one open house had gone well, there was no guarantee that others would be the same. Kelly had enough inventory of brochures, donation forms and one-page summaries of the history of the house. She was going to have to hire more kitchen staff and maintenance people. Jace had done an excellent job, but she couldn't be sure of his continued employment.

The thought of him leaving, however, had her heart sinking. There wasn't enough money at the moment to make the changes she needed, but by this time next year she may be able to afford the racecourse.

"Hi." Ari stood in the doorway. He was wearing his father's jacket.

"Hi," Kelly said. "Who are you? Am I

looking at my little Ari or are you the all grown up Ari?"

He walked in the room, the coat dragging the floor. "I'm the all growed up one."

Kelly smiled. Seeing Ari's sweet face always brightened her day.

"What are you doing?" he asked.

"I'm working on the books."

"Books, like my story books?"

"Not like those," she told him. "These books help me keep track of paying the bills."

"Oh," he said. Kelly knew he had no idea what she meant. "Look here." Kelly pointed at a column of numbers on a piece of paper. Ari put his finger in the same place.

"See that number?"

He bobbed his head up and down.

"That's how much I need to feed the horses."

He looked at Kelly. "I have a paper with how much I need, too."

Ari pulled a folded set of papers from the pocket of his father's jacket. He put his hand on a number and held it up for her to see. "This is how much will feed the horses."

Kelly took the offered pages and looked at them. She held back a gasp when she realized she was looking at the contract of sale for the Kendall. It was a copy. Not the original. Her heart thudded, banging against her chest. Where had Jace gotten this? Straightening the document, the underlined words jumped out at her. *Three years* she read. Then she read the entire clause and saw that it said the original seller had three years to rescind the contract. The tears she'd shed moments ago over being able to support the Kendall, were now tears of gloom. How could Jace do this to her?

For an instant, Kelly wanted to ball the papers up, tear them into confetti-sized pieces and shower the room with them, but she resisted. She needed them intact.

THE CANE MADE a rhythmic cadence on the hardwood floor as Kelly walked down the hall. Her pace was slower than was necessary even with her condition. She was angry and she was doing her best to rein in her emotions.

Reaching the stairs, she put her hand on the railing and ascended one by one. She could hear Jace singing on the upper floor. His voice became louder with each step. He was happy. How could he be? In his bedroom doorway, she stopped and watched. Jace was entertaining Ari, who was sitting, transfixed, on the bed.

At one point, Jace swung around and saw her standing there.

"Kelly, what's wrong?" Jace asked, obviously recognizing how upset she was.

"Ari, could you please go to your room? Maybe look at one of your storybooks?"

"Wow! Good idea."

Once the boy was safely out of earshot, Kelly raised the paper in her hand, and extended it toward Jace.

"What's this?" he asked.

Kelly said nothing. She waited for him to take the papers. He came toward her. Kelly watched every movement as if in slow motion. As he got close enough to her, she moved a finger and the papers fell open. She knew he could read the red underlined words from where he stopped in his tracks.

"I can explain," he said.

"That won't be necessary," she told him. "This speaks for you." She kept her voice calm. While her heart was both breaking and beating as fast as a fan wheel, her body was straight and stiff. She looked the picture of control. "I can't believe you'd betray me like this. You know how much this place means to me. I expect you to pack and leave within the hour."

Kelly didn't wait for him to reply. She turned and moved back to the hall. "I will miss Ari. The horses can stay until you make arrangements for them, but they must be gone by the end of the month."

She left Jace without another word. Kelly limped back to her office and waited for him to go. She flinched fifteen minutes later when she heard the truck doors slam shut and the engine retreat down the driveway. He was out of her sight and no longer a thorn in her side.

Yet her heart bled.

CHAPTER FIFTEEN

SLEEP WASN'T AN OPTION. Kelly knew it when she got in bed at midnight. Now it was three in the morning and she was still awake. The house was empty. She was alone in the huge mansion. And she was well enough to get around without a mishap if she was careful. Mira and Drew had returned to their home. When they left, Kelly hadn't yet found the contract. Mira didn't know Kelly had thrown Jace out. Her cousin wouldn't have let her be alone if she had.

Pushing the covers aside, she got out of bed. Grabbing the cane she'd left leaning against the night table, she stood up. She didn't feel the pain in her leg. That in her heart overrode all other. She went to the kitchen and made herself a cup of coffee. She saw the package Mira used to make the coffee Jace liked. Closing her eyes for a moment, she wondered if everything she saw in the house would remind her of him. How long would it be before the ghost of his presence was no longer part of her routine?

Kelly shook her head. She thought it might be a long time. She wondered about Ari. Was he all right? How had he taken the sudden move? Did he miss her? She didn't even say goodbye to him.

The horses whinnied in the barn. They should be asleep, but they, too, must feel the absence of their friend. She would have to exercise them, feed them and take care of them until Jace returned to collect them or he sent someone else.

The coffee brewed and Kelly took it to her office. It was the one place in the house where she had the least memories of Jace. She opened the desk drawer and found the original contract of sale. She went to the page where the rescind clause was written. She read it. Like the red-lined page on the copy Ari had innocently handed her, *three years* was typed in a black font. She'd read this contract. Her lawyer had read it. How many people in the law office had read it? That she didn't know, but someone must have proofed it. Yet none of them, no one, including herself, had noticed that a line that should have said three months actually read three years.

And now she could possibly be turned out of her own home. She'd been here two years, but she felt the Kendall was more her home than any other place she'd ever lived and that included Short Hills. When she first moved into the mansion, the floors needed refinishing, the walls needed spackling, priming and painting. Some of them she'd had to demolish to the studs and replace. Kelly's sweat was on those walls. It was in every aspect of this house. Her life was in this building. And she wasn't giving it up without a fight.

She pushed the contract aside and did what she'd been trained to do. She developed a plan, created a defense for herself. By six o'clock she'd finished pulling together receipts and organizing them into categories related to the improvements she'd made to the property. She'd kept everything. She knew every penny that had been put into the Kendall, turning it from a run-down failure to the restored glory it was today.

At nine o'clock she called her lawyer and at nine-thirty she was walking into his office with barely a limp.

"This is an unexpected pleasure," Harold Crawford said. "I heard you had a good crowd at the open house. I wish I could have been there, but I was out of town. I'd love to see the old house again."

"Maybe I'll give you a tour if I live there long enough."

He frowned as only a lawyer could. "Did you pull my contract?" she asked.

He lifted the file folder. "We had to get it from the archives. It was just printed and handed to me before you arrived."

"Look at page fifteen," Kelly said.

Harold flipped to the page.

"Third paragraph from the bottom. Line seven." She'd memorized the location. He read for a moment, then looked up at her, clearly distressed.

"It is my belief that Jason Kendall is planning to have the sale rendered null and void."

"Have you spoken to him about this?"

Kelly shook her head. "When I found out I was too angry to do anything except throw him out."

"We'll fight this if he does," Harry said.

"No, Harry, I can't fight. I'm drained." At that point, having no sleep, Kelly felt as if she'd aged ten years. "I poured everything I had into the Kendall. Everything. If he fights me, I can't afford to pay for a defense."

"This is partly my fault. I'll see to it that corrections are made. If Mr. Kendall wants to contest the sale, we'll deal with it."

Kelly stood up and went to the door.

"Kelly," Harry called softly to her. "I remember what happened." He took a moment to scan the papers. Kelly looked at him. "This was the year my secretary was ill. We had a temp in the office—"

"It doesn't matter, Harry," Kelly interrupted him.

"It does matter. Don't worry over this. I'll get in touch with Mr. Kendall's attorney and we'll work it out."

"Thank you."

She was near tears, but she refused to let them fall. This matter wasn't over, but Kelly didn't want to fight Jace. Why did she ever think that she could take control of the Kendall? She'd paid for it fair and square, but even now it felt as if Jace had a better claim than she did. He'd grown up in those rooms. He could raise his son there. They could bring more horses, really bring the place back to what it once was.

Kelly knew that. She'd seen it in Jace's work. He didn't repair and replace the broken fences and everything else like any a contractor. He did it as if he were the owner, as someone who loved what he was doing and who put his heart into it. Kelly felt like a thief taking that away from him. Maybe the error in the contract was there for a reason. She had other options. She could take the job in New York. Perry had said she belonged there. She was good at marketing. She'd get a corner office and a hefty salary that was secure. She could be content with that. She wouldn't have to worry about sales and payroll or upkeep. She could convince the public to buy toasters or electronic gadgets. She could hawk lipstick or show the public how sexy a new car could be.

She could do all those things. She could be happy without the Kendall. It was Jace that she wanted. She didn't think she could be happy without him.

THE NARROW ONE-LANE road that led to the Kendall was at least a mile-and-a-half long, too long for anyone to hear a car heading down it until it was upon the house. Both sides of the road were lined with the white 5-bar gate-style fencing that bordered the lawn on one side and provided access to the parking lot on the other. Kelly came to the door when she heard the heavy sound of engines and truck doors slamming in the driveway.

Her heart lifted when she thought Jace had returned. Through the panes in the door she saw a caravan of three pickup trucks, each attached to double-wide horse trailers. Stepping onto the porch, the heat hit her. A man dressed in jeans and a short-sleeved T-shirt widened his smile when he saw her.

It wasn't Jace. He must have sent someone for the horses, although three trailers for two horses was overkill.

"Ms. Ashton?" one man questioned.

She nodded, coming down the steps. She no longer needed the cane for support.

"I'm Trey Demerest. I have some horses for you."

He shoved some papers toward her. Kelly took them and glanced down. "I don't understand," she said.

"Mr. Jason Kendall said you board horses?"

Kelly stared at the papers, confused. Jace was gone for good. She couldn't ask him about any of this.

"The paperwork is all in order," the man said.

Kelly glanced up.

"Mr. Kendall said you weren't available when he agreed to have us board the horses here, and that you would need to sign the papers, but we thought we'd bring them and you'd agree, we could leave them. He was sure you'd have no problem with anything."

"I think you should know Mr. Kendall is no longer here."

"You still board horses, correct?"

"Yes," Kelly said softly.

"He recommended the Kendall and I'm satisfied with that."

"Give me a chance to look these over," she said.

"Of course," he agreed. "But the boarding fees are here." He pointed to a place at the bottom of page one that went into page two. The fees were reasonable, more than reasonable.

"Mr. Kendall required an account with a

draw for the feed, veterinary services and such. You'll find those details on the next page."

"Who owns these horses?" Kelly asked.

He placed a hand on the cowboy hat he wore and removed it. With a smile of bright white teeth, he said, "I do, ma'am."

"Where were they before? Don't you have a farm?"

He shook his head. "I live in Baltimore, but I love horses. So do my wife and two daughters. The horses were boarded at the Rinkhard farm, but the family is retiring, selling everything and moving to Florida. They asked us to find another place for them. Mr. Kendall recommended this place. I hope everything is all right."

Kelly nodded. "I'm sure it is, but I still need to read this agreement."

Again Trey Demerest smiled. "Mr. Kendall said you'd want to check it out. Do you mind if I see the barn while you do that?"

She smiled in return. "It's around the back." She pointed in the right direction. "If you follow this road, it will end at the barn." Trey and the two other drivers started that way.

Kelly took the contract to the porch and sat in one of the white rocking chairs the tourists had thought were so quaint. She read the agreement. It was above the norm. She didn't know how Jace had gotten them to agree to these details, but the fees were above average, the amount to be drawn would cover even something major and it would be refreshed monthly.

Visitations would be done by prearrangement and was mainly limited to family. If they were to race, the owner would arrange to have them transported to and from the site. Race horses, she thought. These were race horses.

Kelly wanted to cry by the time she got to the end of the agreement. Jace had done this for her. He'd found her horses to board to help with expenses. She would have no out-of-pocket costs. All she needed to do was provide the place for the horses to board. Everything else was taken care of in the agreement. There were six horses; she couldn't exercise them all herself, but there'd be enough funds to cover hiring a groom.

By the time the trio returned, Kelly had finished reading.

"Everything in order?" Trey asked.

"More than in order," she told him. "You do realize the fees in this agreement are above average?" Kelly was a fair person and she wanted to charge a fair price. She didn't want to give the impression that she was cheating or overcharging.

"This is the Kendall," he said. "We negotiated the fees accordingly. I'm comfortable with them. I believe the horses will get the best care here. And I'm willing to pay for it."

Kelly smiled. "About the groom?"

"He's a friend of mine. He's losing his job at the Rinkhard…"

"Emmett Cruz?"

"You know him?" Trey asked.

"Horse country is a small community," she told him. "I know him and I'd be proud if he worked here."

The expression on Trey's face was approving. "Emmett's a natural with horses, likes to be with them all the time."

"I know. There's a small cabin out by the barn. It's livable, but I'll make sure everything is in working order for him."

"Thank you. And if there are any repairs necessary, send me the bill."

"That's very generous," Kelly said.

"So it will work?"

"It will work," she agreed.

Trey produced a pen from inside the truck's cabin and Kelly signed the papers on the hood.

"All right, guys. Let's unload," he instructed.

As they started the trucks and headed for the barn, Kelly watched them, speculating where Jace was. Sadness settled over her. She missed him. More than just wanting to thank him for this incredible gesture, she was used to having him around. She missed seeing him and Ari play in the morning and she missed sitting across from him at the dinner table each night.

She liked the way he smiled, the way he was thorough with his work, yet he took the time to make sure everything was correct. She liked the way his mouth seemed to fit hers as if the two of them were equal halves of the same whole.

The three trucks with trailers, now empty of horses, started back down the one-lane road. Kelly felt bereft. Why hadn't Jace told her he'd done this? Had she given him the chance? She didn't know when he'd met Trey Demerest. Had he been about to tell her when she'd thrown him out?

He could have canceled the contract. Jace had no power to make contracts for the Kendall. He could have called Trey and told him the deal was off.

Yet he hadn't. Kelly would have said Jace wasn't that kind of man. But then she discovered he'd hired an attorney and that her purchase of the Kendall could be null and void. At least it could be rescinded if Jace came up with the tax money. Sheldon would then have to be involved because the property would revert to him, since he was the original owner in this case. Jace could then buy the Kendall from Sheldon, if he could find the means to get a mortgage. Bottom line, to even find out, he would need his brother, since Sheldon was the rightful heir.

And because of the letter Kelly had given him, Jace knew where his brother was.

THE GROCERY STORE, like the hair salon, was the place to hear all the gossip in Windsor Heights. Since Kelly hadn't been in the salon in a while, she opted for the grocery store.

Besides, there'd likely be more people there. Pacing slowly up and down the aisles, picking up milk and bread, condiments and paper products, she scanned the faces of the other customers. She wanted to find someone she knew. Unfortunately, she saw no one who could give her a tidbit of information about Jace.

He'd gone without a word. And while she didn't agree with his tactics or what he might do, she wanted to know where he was and that he and Ari were safe. She also needed to thank him for the extra horses now boarding at the Kendall. Kelly had all kinds of reasons to explain her presence if she could only find him.

Finishing her shopping, she paid the cashier and went to her car. Just as she was about to back out a truck pulled into the space next to hers. Kelly stopped. She hopped out of the car with a huge smile and greeted Emmett Cruz.

"Emmett, great to see you."

"Hello, Ms. Ashton. How are you?"

Kelly shook his hand. "I'm fine. It's so good to see you."

Emmett at one point had been a trainer at

the Kendall when she was a little girl, before he went to work for the Rinkhards. Kelly had been back two years, but between her running the Kendall and Emmett at the Rinkhard place, they saw little of each other.

"I've been meaning to stop by," Emmett said. "I hear you're doing great things over at the Kendall."

"It's going well."

"And I hear one of the Kendalls is back."

Technically true, she thought. "Jason, the wild one."

"Turned up in the middle of the night with a boy."

"I guess horses aren't the only ones you listen to," Kelly joked.

"This is Windsor Heights. Even a toothache will be talked about."

Kelly wondered if she should broach the subject of Jace's whereabouts. Maybe Emmett had heard something.

"He's no longer at the Kendall," Kelly said.

"Yep, heard that, too. Word is you threw him out."

"Does word say why?"

"Nope. Is it true?"

Kelly nodded. "He went behind my back

and hired a lawyer to try to get ownership of the Kendall."

Trey whistled. "Guess that's a good enough reason."

"I don't know where he went. He and Ari, that's the boy's name, left in Drew and Mira's borrowed truck and I haven't heard anything about them since. I owe him a final check and he left two horses with me."

"I've seen the truck about town, but don't know where he's staying. Have you tried the motel out on the highway?"

"I haven't gone looking for him." Kelly's first trip to try to find Jace was today. She'd driven through town hoping to spot the truck, but so far her efforts were a bust.

"Well, if I see him, I'll be sure to tell him you're looking for him."

"No." Kelly spoke too quickly and too loudly. "I mean, I'm not looking for him. I figured he'd contact me sooner or later." Then she added, "About the horses."

Trey was nodding his head.

"What about you? I hear the Rinkhards are planning to sell."

"They are. Not sure when it'll happen

though, or what'll happen to me when it does."

"I know. Trey Demerest brought his horses to board at the Kendall two days ago. In fact, we talked about you."

"Me, why?"

"Trey Demerest recommended you as a groom and I know your work. If you're interested in a new job, you have one at the Kendall. Any idea when the Rinkhards are going to let you know their plans?"

He shook his head.

"Well, come by the Kendall. We'll be waiting for you."

JACE LOOKED DOWN at Ari's head resting on his chest. The boy had fallen asleep on him every night as he sat on the worn sofa in the motel room not five miles from the Kendall. Since they'd left the farm, Ari clung to him. He'd done that in Colombia, but since meeting Kelly he hadn't felt the need.

Ari was unhappy. Jace knew how he felt. Jace must have glanced at the phone a hundred times since he'd driven away from the Kendall. He wanted to call Kelly. He wanted to hear the sound of her voice, smell her hair, hear her laugh and find out how she was doing.

He wanted to be able to explain to Ari why they were no longer at the farm. He wanted to tell him he could go and see Kelly. He wanted to make things right. But he couldn't. He'd done everything he could to push her away. Now there was no going back.

There was one thing Jace wouldn't do. He would not contest the Kendall's sale. Kelly had put her life into its restoration. She hadn't walked the floors or seen the inside of the building until two years ago, but the place was hers. She'd made it hers when she sat on the fence as a child and watched the horses exercising. Taking it away from her now would be the same as killing her. He understood that.

The day of the open house she was more alive than he'd ever seen her. She loved what she was doing. He and Ari would have to go someplace else. Their lives would begin anew, but not with the Kendall as their destination. It had been a stop along the trail, but they would settle someplace else.

Tomorrow Jace would begin to make plans for where they could go. Maybe he'd look up

Sheldon in North Carolina. See if his brother had mellowed in the ensuing years. If he hadn't, they'd move on, but they wouldn't be wanderers. Jace peered down at Ari. His breathing was soft and steady. He pulled the blanket up and over his son and kissed his head. It was just the two of them, as it probably should be. Ari would begin school come September. They needed a place by then. A place far away from the Kendall and from Kelly.

Two days passed, but Jace hadn't been able to find the right moment to talk to Kelly. To let her know his decision to not contest the sale of the Kendall, and that he and Ari were leaving Windsor Heights. He wanted to do all of that face-to-face, and yet whenever he was free, she was busy. He took that as a sign that he was doing the right thing, no matter how much it hurt to be away from Kelly.

FOR THE NEXT couple of days, Kelly worked nonstop. She knew it was too much and so after she returned several phone calls to schedule future events at the Kendall, she went to the barn. There were saddles, tack, harnesses, horse blankets, even names placed on the stable doors for each of the horses. The animals were quiet, but curious. Every horse looked over the open part of its stall door, checking her out. They wanted to know her smell, her attitude. Was she a friendly human or not? They seemed as if they wanted to know if she had treats for them or if she would walk from entrance to exit and ignore their presence.

Horse sense wasn't just a cliche to Kelly. They were smart beasts, strong, loyal and intelligent. She went from one to the other providing carrot sticks and rubbing their noses. Stopping at a stall with the name tag of Stout's Honor written on the placard, she hugged the horse's face and took in the rich, pungent smell.

"So you're a race horse?" she said.

"Yep, I'm a race horse."

Kelly jumped. The sun was behind the man in the doorway, but she'd recognize Emmett's voice anywhere.

"Emmett," she called, already walking toward him.

He caught her in a bear hug and let loose a hearty chuckle. She felt like a kid again.

"I know you've been busy," he said, releasing her. "But I hope to see more of you now that I'll be here."

"You bet you will."

Kelly hugged him again, before standing back and looking at him. "Emmett, I am so glad you're here."

Emmett had to be in his sixties, but he looked twenty years younger. His face had few lines, some around his eyes and the parenthesis markings that framed his mouth.

"Where am I staying?" he asked, using the no-nonsense tone that was his trademark.

"You know where you're staying. And I moved any female trappings." Those were Emmett's words for anything related to women. He'd been married once, had a daughter who was now living in Seattle. After his wife died, he said he could finally remove all the pink and lavender from his life. But Kelly remembered he always had a purple scarf in his pocket at races. A tribute to his late wife.

Arm in arm they strolled through the barn. Emmett already knew the horses, so they didn't give him the same perusal they'd given her.

She opened the door to the cabin and laid the keys in a dish just inside.

"You're perfectly capable of making your own meals, but if you want, breakfast is at seven, lunch at noon and dinner at six. There's hot coffee, cold water in bottles and soft drinks all day. You're always welcome at the main house even if it's outside of those hours."

Emmett nodded.

Kelly turned to go, then recalled something. She turned back. "We have a day when we allow the public to tour the place."

"For a fee?"

"For a fee."

"Good," he approved. "I heard about your first try at that. Susan Johnson came to see me before she went back to Kentucky. Told me you'd done the house proud and made it better, in fact."

Kelly thought of the woman who'd known her father.

"It's open every week on Tuesday. There will be those who want to see the horses. Would you like to handle that or should I hire someone?"

"I'll take care of it," Emmett said.

Kelly was glad it was a job she could delegate to someone else.

"Has Jace not been back?" he asked.

Kelly looked at the floor. "No. He hasn't been back."

Kelly stared at Emmett for a long moment. This was a small town. Emmett must have heard something. "You wouldn't happen to know where he is, would you?"

Emmett shook his head. "The rumor mill hadn't coughed him up yet, but it won't be long. As you said, he's got the kid, and someone is bound to see him. You want me to tell Jace you asked when I find out?"

Kelly's head snapped up. She did, but she couldn't say that. "I want to thank him. Having the other horses here will help a lot with the finances and with bringing the Kendall back to where it was."

"Is that all?"

The way he asked the question said he knew there was something between her and Jace. It wasn't exactly true.

But it wasn't false, either.

CHAPTER SIXTEEN

SHELDON KNOCKED OFF for the day. Going back to his bungalow, he took a long, hot shower and dressed in clean shorts and a shirt. It was wash day, so he gathered his clothing, stuffed it in a canvas bag and headed to the Laundromat. Not far from the marina was a place where the sailboat owners could wash towels and the various items that proved sea duty was a dirty business. Christian fell in step with him as he headed toward it. The marina was in the opposite direction of where he lived.

"Hi," he said. The boy was carrying a book.

"Where are your friends?" Sheldon asked.

He knew he went to camp each weekday and that he often played with some of the kids farther up the beach.

"My best friend went away last night to visit his father. His parents are divorced." He said it with an authority beyond his years.

"He's not your only friend. Where are the others?"

"Most are playing video games. They say it's too hot to do anything but swim and play games."

"Swimming is good. Why aren't you doing that?"

"Too many grown-ups in the pool." Christian frowned.

"What have you got there?" Sheldon referred to the book in the boy's hand.

Christian, never breaking stride, held it out so Sheldon could read the cover. "*Chet, the Cowboy,*" Sheldon said out loud.

"They make us read at least a book every two weeks at camp."

Sheldon nodded. He was impressed and thought that was a good idea. "What else do you do at camp?"

"Most of it is fun. We go to a park and play baseball and basketball. We swim, watch movies. I take a class on how to use my camera."

"That does sound like fun. Where's the camera?"

Christian pulled a small digital camera

from his back pocket and held it up for Sheldon to see.

"Have you learned how to use it?"

"Yeah," he said. "All you have to do is look through here." He indicated the viewfinder. "And press this button."

"I'm sure there's more to it than that."

"There is, but I haven't learned it yet."

"So you're reading and taking pictures?"

"I have to bring the pictures to camp. I take the camera and they use the card inside to get the pictures off. Can I take one of you?"

Sheldon grinned. "Sure," he said.

Christian was already moving the camera up to look at the small screen. Sheldon stood still. He was considerably taller than his photographer. Changing his mind, he sat on the ground and crossed his long legs, and looked straight at the camera.

Christian snapped a picture. Then he moved several steps and took another. Again, several more steps, this time to the side, and snapped a photo.

"Enough," Sheldon announced, getting to his feet. "I'm not that interesting. What about the marina. The boats there are beautiful and would be good subjects for you."

"I already took a lot of those," he said.

The two began walking again. "Have you taken some of your friends?"

"Yeah," he said as if he'd exhausted all the subjects he knew. "My grandma, too."

"What about buildings? There are some cool houses around here. There are the stores in town. You could choose one subject and take a lot of that type. Do a study of it."

"What do you mean?" Christian frowned up at him, screwing his face into a peculiar mask.

"Well, you could choose windows and take pictures of the windows in a lot of places, stores, houses, boats, cars. Or you could choose doors, roofs, cars..."

"Cars," he stopped Sheldon. "I like cars."

"There are some terrific ones around here. But," he cautioned, "if you see the owner, be sure to ask permission first."

"I will."

They reached the Laundromat. Sheldon held the door and his small charge went inside. While the dryers produced heat, it was still cooler inside than out. Sheldon went directly to the washers. He was familiar with this place, coming once a week to clean his clothes. Once he put the clothes in the machine, he lifted Christian onto it and the two of them sat and waited for the clothes to be washed.

"You wanna know what else we do at camp?" Christian asked.

"I'd love to." Sheldon smiled. He hadn't had much interaction with children in his past and he found he loved hearing about the world through the eyes of this nine-year-old. Everything was wonderful and new. It was like he discovered the world every time he turned a corner.

"We were playing a game one day when it was raining and we couldn't go to the park."

"So what did you do?"

"We talked about places."

"What places?"

"A lot of them. Our counselor is from way up north in Canada and he told us about where he was born and what they grow and eat there. Then he asked us what we knew about where we lived."

"What did you tell him?"

"I didn't know a lot." He twisted around and looked at Sheldon. "I told them about the beach and that there were a lot of fish in the ocean. That there were sea shells in the sand and sometimes we collected them and made things. I told him there were a lot of boats in the water and that you cleaned the bottoms."

"You told them about me?"

"Was that all right?" Immediately, Christian was defensive.

"Yes, that was all right." He reassured him.

"I told them that the boats couldn't go very fast if you didn't take care of them."

Sheldon smiled. That wasn't exactly the truth, but for a nine-year-old to distill it to that level was fine.

"Tell me about where you're from," Christian asked.

Sheldon thought about that. Could he really say he was from somewhere? Maryland felt like a lifetime ago.

"I could tell you the history of Maryland, but that would be boring."

Christian laughed. "Tell me about where you lived before you came here." He looked up at Sheldon as if he was ready to hang on every word.

"Before coming here I'd lived in a lot of places. But I'm from Maryland. I lived on a farm there. We called it the Kendall."

"It was named after you?" Christian sat up straighter as he asked the question, impressed that someone could have a farm with his name on it.

"Not after me. I come from a long line of Kendalls. The farm was named by one of those long-ago relatives."

"I've never seen a farm. I mean never been on one. We drove by farms when I came to live with my grandma. But I don't really remember any names of them."

"It wasn't a farm that grew anything except grass."

"Grass?" Again he screwed his face into a frown.

"It was a horse farm."

"Horses!" This caused a huge smile to replace the frown. "How do you farm horses?"

"We bred them, meaning we raised the horses from the time they were born. We boarded them, let them live in a long stable."

"Did you get to ride them?"

"Every day," Sheldon clarified. "Horses have to be exercised so they don't get fat and have problems with their legs."

"Like I have to go to gym in school."

"Exactly." Sheldon smiled at his comprehension.

"Who's exercising the horses now?"

Sheldon frowned. "I had to sell the horses before I left."

Christian thought about that for a while. Then he perked up and looked Sheldon directly in the face. "I suppose you couldn't leave them alone. Someone would need to give them food and water and exercise them."

"Exactly," Sheldon said. At that moment the washer finished its cycle.

SHELDON LISTENED TO their footsteps as he and Audrey walked from the theater later that night. They'd gone to the movies. He'd taken her on a date. He hadn't been out with another woman since Laura died.

"Christian told me you told him about your farm in Maryland."

"He mentioned his camp project. I gave him some information to share."

"That was nice of you. He's been talking about horses since you mentioned them. He asked me to take him to the library so he could get some books."

Sheldon smiled.

"You're a good influence on him."

"Thank you," Sheldon said. "I wasn't a good influence on my own brother."

"Life gives us second chances," Audrey said.

"Is that written on a card in your classroom?" he asked.

"It is," she said. "That doesn't mean it's not true."

"I have a letter from Jason," he said.

Audrey stopped on the street and faced him. She seemed too surprised to speak. "Why didn't you tell me? You said it like you were asking to pass the butter, when contacting him has plagued you for months."

"I haven't opened it."

"Why not?"

"Fear." He paused for a long time. "I don't know what's in it. He doesn't know me now, doesn't know where I've been and what I've gone through. The letter could tell me to never contact him again."

"It could," she agreed. "But you'll never know what it says if you don't open it."

"I realize that."

"How did he find you?" Audrey asked.

"I sent a letter to the Kendall as you suggested. I never expected to get a response from Jason." Sheldon thought he might get a reply from the owner of the farm, but seeing Jason's handwriting and the return address on the envelope, it nearly burned his hand. "I assume he lives at the Kendall. He must be doing well if he could return to the Kendall and support the farm."

"Don't jump to any conclusions. You only know that Jason used the address."

"How many people are you aware of who would allow you to use their address if you didn't live there?"

She nodded, understanding his point. "But when you left, you said the place was run-down."

"It was, but someone bought it. A woman. I have no idea what it looks like now."

"It could have been sold to your brother," she suggested.

"Which means he'd have to have enough money to purchase it."

"That's beside the point, isn't it. You're not interested in his finances. You want to contact him for different reasons."

Sheldon looked away. She was right. He

did want to contact his brother to try to make amends.

"I don't think I can just apologize and our past antagonism will up and disappear. There's a lifetime of bad blood between us, which I caused."

Audrey took his arm. Her fingers moved down until she reached his hand, which she caught and held. "Nothing is ever that absolute. Even if you don't make amends with your brother, you'll be better for trying. It's up to you. If attempting to explain your actions because not doing it is holding your stomach in knots, then they will never go away until you do something about it."

Sheldon pulled her arm through his and the two continued walking. Instead of him taking her to her porch, he passed it and continued to the bungalow where he'd lived for the past eight months.

The place was only three rooms and a bath. Sheldon kept it neat, he didn't have much. He swept daily, cleaned his dishes and made his bed.

"Have a seat," he said when she came inside. "I have iced tea or I can make coffee or there's bottled water." Sheldon didn't have any alcohol. He'd given it up for a lot of good reasons. "What can I get you?"

"Iced tea would be good," she said.

Sheldon poured two glasses of tea and set them on the small table in the kitchen. While Audrey drank hers, he retrieved the envelope with Jason's name on it. Both of them looked at the letter. Audrey said nothing. The only sound in the room was their breathing. Outside, Sheldon heard the marina water lapping against the pier and the gentle bobbing of boats as they rose and fell with the ever shifting bay.

Sheldon slid his finger under the flap and opened the envelope. Inside was a single sheet of paper. He pulled it out and read it, then passed it to Audrey who read it, too.

Sheldon moved to the window and looked out on the marina.

I'm back. I live at the Kendall. Why are you looking for me?

One line, three sentences. That was all he said. The words gave him no indication of anything about Jason.

"He doesn't say much," Audrey said.

"That's the way it was with us. If we

weren't arguing, we weren't saying anything at all."

"Are you going to answer his question?" Audrey asked.

"I don't know. I wrote the note to the Kendall, but to be truthful I thought it was a waste of time. I didn't expect an answer. When the reply came, I thought Jason would say something other than he was living at the farm."

"I know you need to think on this and you need to make a decision," Audrey said. "I have to check on Christian."

Sheldon knew she had a sitter and a promised return time. "I'll walk you home." Sheldon escorted her to her house in silence. His mind was on Jason and the glory days of his past. It hurt to think of them now. Not because of his circumstances, but because he wished he'd been the man he was today back then.

Outside Audrey's door, she said, "Have you thought of returning? Looking your brother in the face and telling him how you feel?"

Sheldon stared at her. "I've thought of it," he said. Then he said good-night and turned to walk back.

He knew the decision he needed to make.

He had to confront Jason and work out whatever was necessary, if Jason would even
allow it. If he didn't, Sheldon would accept
that.

But it was a task that had to be done.

THE DAY BEFORE the first wedding ever to be
held at the Kendall was filled with activity.
Kelly didn't have time to think of her feelings
much. She was too busy directing the preparations—the placement of tables and chairs,
making sure everything was in order. Kelly
had been lucky enough to find a hotel selling its old tables, chairs and parquet dance
flooring. She could handle parties up to three
hundred, which is what the ballroom would
hold. The wedding consultant arrived and
with the small army of temps Kelly had on
hand, they transformed the ballroom into a
reception hall. All the tables and chairs were
covered in white. The chairs had huge bows
on their backs. The color scheme for the napkins was blush and hot pink. Tomorrow the
florist would deliver the centerpieces and
bouquets for the wedding party.

The bride wanted to use the main staircase for the procession and photos. The baker

would arrive with the cake and the caterers would take over the kitchen right after breakfast. When everything was done and Kelly was finally alone, she put her feet up to rest her ankle, which had swollen again.

Now that her mind had a chance to slow down, her thoughts returned to Jace and Ari. Despite the pain in her leg, she grabbed her cane and went to the horse barn. The horses always made her feel closer to them. She went to the mare Jace had ridden and rubbed his nose.

"I miss him, too," she told the horse. She hadn't heard from Jace in days. She missed watching the two of them every morning. She missed hearing Ari scampering through the house. She missed their presence of being on the property. The place was too quiet. Inside and outside, she felt lonely.

Moving to the other mare, she rubbed his nose, too. Kelly had ridden them that morning before all the activity started, but she had the feeling the horses knew that Ari and Jace were no longer on the property.

Her leg was really hurting and her limp was prominent. If she was going to be of any use tomorrow, she needed to get off her foot. Leaving the barn, she hobbled back to the house. She didn't feel like eating, so she bypassed the kitchen. It was set up for the caterers anyway and she didn't want to disturb anything. Limping around the porch, she headed for the front of the house. When she turned the corner, she saw Jace.

She froze, a gasp escaped before she could stop it.

Jace heard her and turned toward the sound. The cane Kelly was using slipped out of her hand and fell to the floor. She didn't make a move to catch or retrieve it. Her eyes were glued to the man standing twenty feet away.

She was happy to see him. Every part of her reacted to him. She felt her body tremble. He'd returned. He'd come back. Then she realized he was on his own. Ari was not with him. Kelly looked to the truck, but the child was not there. Jace had not come back. He wasn't here for the horses, either. There was no trailer in sight.

The only other reason would be to serve her legal papers. At least he didn't have them come by mail or delivered by a clerk from some law office.

"Are you here about the contract?" she asked.

He shook his head.

"Where's Ari?"

"He's visiting a day-care school," Jace supplied.

"So you're planning to stay in the area?" Of course he would stay, she thought. He was challenging her for the house. She was the one who'd eventually move.

"We haven't really decided."

Then why was he here? Kelly wondered. "You must want your last paycheck." Forgetting that her ankle was swollen, she took a step. Pain shot to her knee and she crumpled to the porch floor.

"Kelly!" Jace called and rushed to her. His arms were around her and he was pulling her up before he knew it. He examined her ankle. "What have you done? We need to get some ice on this. And in a hurry."

Jace lifted Kelly and carried her into the house. He took her upstairs and to the first bathroom he found. Rolling her pant legs up, he set her on the bathtub rim and turned the cold water on. "Keep your feet in here. I'll get some ice."

He left her and came back moments later with ice wrapped in a dish towel. He set the towel on the sink counter and turned the water off. Taking a dry towel, he turned her around and dried her feet. Kelly winced at his touch, more from his hands than pain.

"What's going on in the kitchen?" he asked.

"We have a wedding tomorrow," she told him.

"You didn't set up all those tables I saw in the ballroom, did you?"

She shook her head. "I had staff do that, but I helped with the linens and tying of the bows."

"And that caused the swelling?"

She nodded.

"Does it feel better," Jace asked.

"I'm fine," Kelly insisted.

"I know." He took the ice pack and put it on her ankle, then wrapped that in a dry towel and secured it with a couple of rubber bands. "Here, take these."

He had two small white pills in his hand.

"What are they?"

"The pain pills the doctor gave you."

"They make me sleepy," Kelly said, but she took them along with the glass of water he'd set on the counter.

"You could use some sleep." Jace picked her up again and took her to her bedroom.

He sat on the bed and took her hand. Kelly closed hers around his. She liked the feel of it in hers. He had a strength that she seemed to draw whenever he was near. Kelly didn't know how long he sat there. She was getting woozy from the medication.

"I have to get Ari," he said, standing up and taking a step back.

His retreat hurt her more than any injury to her ankle. Yet she didn't blame him. And it certainly wasn't his fault that she'd not used her cane when she should have.

"Sure," she said. "Don't worry about me. Ari needs you. Tell him I said hello." Her voice sounded far away.

"You'll keep the ice on it like I said?"

"Yes," she replied. Jace turned to leave. As he reached the door, Kelly said, "Tell Ari I miss him."

"I'll be back," he said.

Though she hadn't orchestrated it, she was glad to see Jace again. She should have known better than to overdo things and have her leg swell up, especially since she had a wedding planned for the following day.

Thankfully tomorrow she'd have little more to do than unlock the door. The wedding consultant was efficient. She'd gone over with Kelly all the places the bride and groom would need to complete their ceremony, reception and photo shoot.

Kelly didn't hear the door close. She was already asleep.

When Kelly opened her eyes again, she had the feeling a lot of time had gone by. She turned over. The ice on her leg had disappeared. The swelling had gone down and her leg no longer throbbed with pain. Her cousin sat in a chair reading.

"Mira? What are you doing here?"

Dropping the magazine she'd been engrossed in, she looked up. "A little bird told me you'd pushed yourself too hard."

"You saw Jace? He was really here?"

"You don't remember?" Mira asked.

She was still a little disoriented from the medication. She looked at her hand. Jace had held it. That was the last thing she remembered.

She sat up. "I remember now. He put ice on my ankle."

"And he called me."

"I'm sorry. I'm all right."

"Obviously now you are," Mira reprimanded. "I know you want everything perfect here, but if you're not careful that injury could sideline you for a longer time than it needs to."

"Sideline?" Kelly said with raised eyebrows.

"Sorry," she said. "Too much Drew and his football analogies. Nevertheless, the statement still stands."

"It probably won't matter much," Kelly said, her voice resigned.

"What does that mean?"

Kelly pulled her pillows up and leaned back against them. She told Mira all of what had happened in the past few weeks. From the moment Jace had shown up on her doorstep until she threw him out five days ago. The only points she left out were the several kisses they'd shared and how his touch made her feel like a queen.

"And you think he's only here to take the Kendall from you?" Mira asked.

"He pretty much came straight out and told me."

"But then things changed." Mira spoke as if she knew something Kelly didn't.

"What?"

"You and Jace," she said. "Don't tell me you're not in love with him."

Kelly stared straight ahead. She nodded so slightly, Mira may not have seen it, but Kelly knew her cousin was perceptive.

"His affection for me could have another purpose," Kelly pointed out.

"Like what?"

"Like he would change his tactics to get the Kendall back."

"And he's romancing you in order to get you to sign the place over to him?" It sounded incredible.

"It's not outside the realm of possibility," Kelly said.

"Unless you're inside a Victorian novel."

Kelly was beginning to feel exasperated. "What do you suggest his motives are?" Kelly asked.

"I think he's head over heels in love with you."

"I don't think so."

"Why, because he's never said it?"

"That's one reason."

"Maybe because you put up walls," Mira offered.

Kelly didn't deny that. "I know you've had bad experiences in the past. I know that guy Streeter showed up here at the open house and he was the last person you needed to see, but none of us get through life without kissing a toad or two. It's necessary so we know a prince when we find one."

"You can't believe Jace is a prince?" Kelly questioned.

"He's not my prince. You have to decide if he's yours."

JACE MET ARI at the day care, but they didn't go back to Kelly's. Both of them jumped into the truck and headed for nowhere in particular. Jace did, however, call Mira and she told him Kelly's condition. He couldn't take the chance of seeing Kelly again.

Once Ari was with all the kids and toys at the day-care center, he'd dropped Jace's hand and ran for them and the director said he could stay for a couple of hours, that Jace was then free to do what he wanted.

And what he wanted then was to see Kelly. He wanted to talk to her, but she was in pain from her leg. Going back would mean he was bound to blurt his feelings out. And what would she think? That he was merely trying to get the Kendall by pretending to love her?

Jace was in love with her. But look at the mess he'd made of everything. Nothing had gone right since he'd driven into town and asked Kurt Mallard for a loan. He'd told himself he was doing it for Ari, doing it to get his home back for his son. And while that was partially true, it had changed as he got to know Kelly. He'd never seen a stronger woman. She loved the Kendall. She loved everything about it, every nail, every tile. And she'd work herself to death to restore it.

Jace wondered if he would have felt that way. Had he inherited the house and grounds when his father died, would he have put as much heart and devotion into restoring it as Kelly had? He'd like to say he would, but the truth was he wasn't sure. He wanted the place to remain a good home for his son. He wanted to live here and make it the happy place he knew it could be. But now he wanted to make it that home with not just Ari, but with Kelly, as well.

"Did you like the school?" Jace asked his son.

"It was awesome," Ari said. "I can go back again?"

Jace nodded. "You can go back."

Ari was so happy, he hummed along to the radio without a care in the world. For a while he would forget about missing Kelly. What Jace wouldn't give to be in his shoes.

CHAPTER SEVENTEEN

DREW STOOD UP from the task of cutting the grass as Jace drove up to the man's house. Ari was ensconced in the day-care center, which had become his favorite place to go. He even forgave his dad for not continuing his riding lessons since they left the Kendall. He still asked about Kelly, but he didn't do it a hundred times a day. Only half that many.

Mira appeared in the doorway as Jace stepped down from the cab. "This is a surprise," she said, smiling.

Drew joined his wife and the two of them met Jace. "What's up?" Drew asked.

"I thought I should return your truck." Jace lifted his hand and held the keys out to Drew. He didn't move to take them.

"Are you leaving town?"

"Not sure," he said.

"How are you going to get around if you return the truck?" Mira asked.

"Since I'm no longer at the Kendall, it seemed like the right thing to do," Jace explained.

"But how are you going to get around?" she asked again.

Jace shrugged. "I'll manage. I can rent a car for a while or—"

"Do you have a job?" Drew interrupted.

"Not yet, but I'm looking. There is plenty I can do."

"That's not the point," Drew said.

Mira took Drew's arm. "What my husband means is, the truck is not being used, so you can keep it as long as you're here."

"Whether you're at the Kendall or not," Drew clarified.

Jace smiled. Drew and Mira were good people. "Thank you."

"Now that that's settled, want some coffee or iced tea?" Mira asked with a wide grin.

"Since I miss your coffee, I'll have that." He smiled.

She looked at Drew.

"Iced tea," he said.

The three of them sat at an umbrella table and drank their beverages.

"Have you decided what you're going to do?" Drew asked.

Jace shook his head back and forth.

"What about the Kendall?" Mira asked. "Are you going to contest the sale?"

"You heard what happened?" Jace frowned.

"Kelly told us."

"I'm not contesting it," he said.

"Kelly thinks you are," Drew told him. "It would hurt her tremendously if you negate all her hard work."

"I know. I couldn't do that to her," Jace said. "Ari would never get over it…and neither would I."

"She'll be glad to hear that," Mira said.

"Please don't tell her," Jace rushed to say. "I want to do it. She should hear it from me."

Husband and wife nodded.

"Why wouldn't you stay around here?" Mira wanted to know.

"It would be hard to do that."

"You mean with everyone knowing you are a Kendall and that you no longer own the farm?" Drew asked.

"I never owned the Kendall," he said. "I never had any right to it."

"Except a moral one," Drew said. "Your father did you an injustice by not including you in his will."

"It was what he did while I was alive," Jace said. "I didn't expect anything different at his death. It's done and can't be undone. Not by me at any rate."

Sheldon had that right, but Jace would no longer undermine Kelly.

Jace stood up then. There was nothing more to say. "Well, I have to go but, thank you for the use of the truck." He was about to leave when Drew stood up. The men shook hands and Jace nodded at Mira. He started for the truck as Drew went back to cutting the grass.

"Come by sometime and bring Ari," Mira called to Jace, following him to the truck.

"I will. He loves those cakes you make." He got inside the truck and closed the door.

"Why don't you tell her?" Mira asked.

"That I'm not going to sue for ownership?"

"That you're in love with her."

Jace looked through the front windows, then back at Mira. He could lie, but it was no use. If she knew, if she could see how he felt about Kelly just by looking at him, there was no point in denying her words.

"She wouldn't believe me," he said.

KELLY TRIED TO concentrate, but she couldn't. She'd been in her office, but left it to wander about the mansion. Even with the rain pelting the windows, the place was silent. She stopped at the patio door and looked out. The garden Jace and Ari built for her made her lonely for them. In the distance on one side was the gazebo. It was completely outlined in white lights that made a dramatic statement in the darkness. On the other side was the stable. The mares were still there, but their owner was nowhere to be seen.

Kelly was thankful the wedding was yesterday. It went off without a hitch. The sun shone brightly. It was beautiful, a perfect day for a couple to begin their lives together. She'd watched the bride come down the staircase. She'd never seen a wedding so artistically arranged. And she couldn't help but imagine herself dressed all in white coming down those same steps. Tears had gathered in her eyes and she knew if she remained in the room looking at the happy couple, she would cry. As the groom took the bride's hand in front of the minister and he started the vows, Jace came to mind and Kelly fled the ceremony.

When the sound of applause reached her, she knew the groom had just kissed the bride. Moments later she heard footsteps as the guests made their way to the ballroom. The wedding party had gone to have pictures taken.

A clap of thunder brought her attention back to the window. Kelly limped to her office. On the conference table, she picked up a folder, then went to her desk and propped her foot up. Checking the calendar, she saw that the next open house was three days away. She opened the folder and went over the plans. The crews were all ready. They'd broken down the rooms after the wedding and would come in the morning to prepare them for the open-house guests.

Flipping to the next page in the folder, Kelly saw the wedding plan and yesterday returned to her mind.

She'd watched the bride and groom from her office window, the same one that was now covered in rainwater. The couple loved horses and wanted photos in their wedding attire with them. Kelly pictured them and the photographer as they posed with the two mares. The wedding planner had told her that both bride and groom loved horses and that was the main reason they'd contracted to have their wedding at the Kendall.

Silently, Kelly thanked Jace for bringing the horses to the Kendall. Shaking her head she tried to dislodge him from her mind, but he refused to be assuaged. She saw the white gown and veil extending outward. But it wasn't yesterday's bride and groom that she saw. It was a little boy and his father romping along the back lawn. This time when the tears came, she let them fall.

Kelly didn't know how long she stayed there, absentminded of anything going on around her. When she became aware of her surroundings, she realized the phone was ringing. Kelly dried her eyes with a tissue, took a long sobering breath and reached for the receiver. "Kendall Farm, this is Kelly Ashton," she said without a trace of sadness in her voice.

For twenty minutes she spoke with a woman about a booking for a fiftieth wedding anniversary party for her parents. It sounded like an extravagant event and the Kendall would be a perfect venue for it. When Kelly replaced the receiver, she was no longer melancholy. The woman had reminded her to concentrate on the business at hand.

Kelly went over the rest of the plans for the next open house, checking off the jobs that had been completed. She could think of nothing that might be missing. Kelly was getting to know the regional suppliers and they were doing a fine job for her. She knew the success of the Kendall meant more income for the businesses associated with it. People would stop to eat in town or buy gasoline. Some might stay at the local motel or hotel.

She had business cards and flyers for local services in case someone asked for information on something they discovered at the Kendall. The gift shop was more profitable than she'd thought it would be. She smiled, thinking of the work Jace had done building the gift shop. When she walked through it after he'd done the remodeling, she'd touched every wall and window, proud that what she imagined was now real. And proud that Jace had been there to help with the creation. As much as he said he wanted no part of opening the house to the public, he'd realized the advantages of making it happen. Even returning on that first day and pitching in to help her.

Then she remembered waking up the next morning in her bed. She knew he'd carried her there. Ari had confirmed it for her, although she had a vague memory of floating through the air. She thought it had been a dream at first, but logic told her she didn't walk to her bed and sleep in her clothes.

She missed Jace and wondered where he was.

SHELDON KENDALL IV stood at the end of the long drive. Trees lined both sides of the white fence. It was a different fence, he thought. The mailbox with Kendall Farm printed on it in red letters had also been changed. The old crooked one sitting askew on a rusting post had been replaced with a large white replica of the house. It sat sideways on the post with the doors open to accept the mail.

Cars constantly turned at one end of the property and drove down a paved road that hadn't been there two years ago. Sheldon thought this must be one of many changes he'd encounter. Never had he expected to be here. But he'd come this far. He had to go the last mile. He may be leaving today with more scars than expected, but he knew he had to take this journey to its conclusion.

Another car passed him, driving too fast along the narrow road. He felt the wind whip through his secondhand suit in the aftermath of the car's speed. Sheldon had shaved and had his hair cut for the trip. By the time he reached the end of the road, he'd removed the suit jacket and carried it over his arm. People were getting out of cars and crossing through a gate, then going to a small station on the side before heading up the seven steps that led to the large porch and the front door.

"What is going on?" he wondered.

Heading for the same small house, he looked inside.

"Ticket, sir?" a young blonde girl asked. She looked about nineteen.

"Ticket?" he questioned. What would he need a ticket for?

"For the tour? It's $35.00."

Sheldon calculated how many groceries he could buy for $35.00. He shook his head. "Is the owner here?" he asked.

"Ms. Ashton. I don't know where she is. I'll give her a call if you like."

"I'd appreciate it."

"What's your name?" the blonde asked.

Sheldon told her, just giving his first name.

The girl made a call on a cell phone. After a moment, she began to speak. Her head snapped up at him. "Sheldon *Kendall*?" she asked.

He nodded.

Then she was back at the phone. A second later, she clicked if off and said, "Please go to the front door." She pointed the way as if he didn't know.

When he arrived there, a redhead was smiling at the guests going in and then she approached him.

"Sheldon Kendall?"

"Yes. I'm looking for Jason. I got a letter saying he's living here."

"I'm Kelly Ashton."

"Are you the new owner?"

"I am. Let's go somewhere more quiet." She walked to the end of the porch, away from the crowds. "Jace isn't here anymore. I'm sorry, but I don't know where he went."

Sheldon's disappointment was telling. He

gazed out at the lush lawn. It looked wonderful.

"Have you traveled all the way from North Carolina without telling him you were coming?"

"The letter I got is only a few weeks old. He said he was here."

"He was, but he and Ari left about three weeks ago."

"Ari?"

"His son. I guess he didn't tell you about the boy, either?" Kelly said.

"His letter was very short." It was so short that Sheldon could interpret little if anything from it.

"Why don't you come inside and have something to eat and drink. And I'll make some calls."

"Thank you." Sheldon had nothing else to say. He couldn't just turn around and go back to the bus station. In any case, there wasn't another bus until tomorrow night at the earliest. He adjusted the knapsack on his shoulder.

Kelly pointed to the parking lot. "As you can see we're having an open house today."

"Open house?"

"It's a long story and Jace didn't agree with

it, but I offer paid tours of the house and grounds to the public. People love history, especially when there are period costumes and furnishings to see." She started walking. Sheldon followed her. "I'll cordon off the upstairs rooms for us."

"I'm sure that will be fine."

Kelly led him through the front door. At the grand staircase, she secured the velvet cord after the two of them went up the first step. At the top of the stairs, Sheldon looked back. There was a lot of coming and going. He remembered the parties they used to have when his father was alive. The foyer would be full of women in fancy dresses and men in formal attire. Now he looked at people wearing shorts and T-shirts with earbuds hanging around their necks.

"Sheldon?"

He caught up to Kelly. "You're perfectly welcome to join a tour, or you can wait in this room until we find out where Jace is. He told me it was yours."

Sheldon stepped inside his old bedroom and the rest of the world receded.

"I'll get you something to eat," Kelly said. "Is there something in particular you'd like?"

"Anything would be fine. Thank you."

She smiled and closed the door.

Nothing had changed and everything had changed. The paint was different. Curtains replaced the heavy drapes that used to hang at the windows. The bed was the same, although the covers were new. The whole room was brighter. There was a small table sitting in front of the fireplace. He remembered it well. In fact, he could recall the dates of all the antique furniture. He knew when renovations had been done prior to his leaving. Obviously, from what he'd seen from the foyer to this bedroom, other changes had also been completed.

Sheldon's room was huge and looked out one side of the house. In all the years he'd lived here, he'd never moved to the master bedroom, but preferred to remain in the room where he'd grown up. It had been redecorated. Laura had done that once, but her changes were gone now. The bed, a giant four-poster, sat between the windows. The fireplace was on the left with a sitting area in front of it.

This was once Sheldon's home. But nothing about him remained in it today. He didn't own the Kendall. Jason didn't own it. Jason wasn't even here. And he had a son.

What did Sheldon have other than regrets?

KELLY HAD TO stop and think. Her jaws were clenched so tight, her back teeth ached. Sheldon's arrival was the last thing she needed today.

With so many people all over the house, his being here only added to the confusion, when a clear mind was essential to deal with the guests and staff.

What was he doing here, showing up unannounced? Had Jace asked him to come?

Forcing herself to relax, Kelly walked slowly down the back stairs, leading to the kitchen. She clutched the handrail due to her wobbly legs. Were the brothers joining together against her? Jace told her he wanted the property for him and Ari. Was Sheldon here to support that goal?

"What's wrong?" Mira asked.

Her voice drew Kelly's attention.

"You look like a ghost."

"Sheldon Kendall is here," Kelly said.

"Why?"

"I have no idea. I literally found him on the doorstep."

"What did he say?" Mira asked.

"So far, nothing significant. He wants to talk to Jace."

"Where is Jace?"

"I don't know."

That was her problem. She had no answers for the questions that crowded in on her.

"Where is Sheldon now?"

"Upstairs, in one of the bedrooms. I came to get him something to drink."

Mira reached for a pitcher of water and a glass. "What happens next?"

Kelly shook her head. "I suppose I'm going to have to ask him and Jace what's going on."

JACE AND ARI came out of the day-care center and Jace strapped his son into his car seat. Whistling, Jace pulled his tie loose and laid his suit jacket on the cab's seat. He had good news for the boy. He decided to take him to the ice-cream shop to celebrate while he told him.

Walking around Drew and Mira's truck, he jumped as he recognized Emmett Cruz's SUV coming straight at him. Emmett drove wildly across the road, roaring to a stop as he blocked him in. The short man jumped out of the vehicle clearly looking for someone.

Jace had heard that Emmett was working at the Kendall. "Emmett, there could be kids out here. Be careful."

"Sorry," Emmett said. "I've been searching for you for the past half hour."

Immediately Jace's mind went to Kelly.

"What's up?" Jace asked. He stood beside the truck, blocking the door, protecting his son from whatever might be happening.

"Kelly sent me to find you."

"Why? Is she all right?"

"It's not her exactly. But she does need you to return to the Kendall as fast as possible."

"Why?" Jace asked.

"Just come."

Emmett was a man of few words. He preferred horses to people. He got back in his SUV and pulled away. He drove slowly until he was out of the parking lot, then the truck zoomed up the road as if it was late for something important.

Jace got in his truck and headed in the same direction. What could Kelly want? First, she asked him to leave, now she sent

Emmett looking for him and wouldn't say why. When Jace eventually turned into the Kendall's long driveway, Ari let out a shout.

"We're home!" the boy said, with obvious happiness. Jace didn't have the heart to say a thing.

Out front was a sign for visitors' parking and the procession of cars told him the open house was well under way. He parked by the stables, away from the flow of visitors and next to Emmett's SUV. The moment he released Ari from his car seat, the boy took off running for the house and calling Kelly's name. Jace took a slower route, entering through the garden he'd built under her office window.

Of all the noises in the building, people talking, guides explaining, Jace heard Ari. He followed the boy's excited voice to Kelly's office. She turned and looked at him. She'd changed her hair. It was swept up off her neck and coiled around her head. Sunlight poured through the window, forming a red halo around her.

Jace swallowed. He started across the room, coming to a stop so close that he could reach out and easily pull her into his arms.

"I'm going to go on the tour with Amy," Ari said, scampering away. He slammed the door as he left.

Jace stared at Kelly. He hadn't realized how much he could miss seeing someone. He wanted to kiss her, long and hard.

"You wanted me," he said. His voice was several notes lower than usual.

Her eyes opened a little wider. Jace realized what he'd said, but he didn't take it back.

"I wanted…" She stopped and looked down.

Jace wanted to reassure her, so he waited. He'd wait forever for Kelly.

"You wrote to your brother," she said.

Jace nodded without thinking. How could she know that? He hadn't told her.

"He's here," Kelly said.

"What? Why?"

"I don't know. He showed up an hour ago asking for you."

All the old taunts came back to Jace. The insults and comments on how he wasn't a true Kendall. How he was an illegitimate child with no home and no one to love him. How their father only let him live there to keep tongues from wagging. But he didn't want him there, which was why they were always sending him away.

"He's in his old room," Kelly told him. She paused a moment, scrutinizing him.

Jace had told her some of the things that happened when he was younger, but no one who hadn't experienced it could truly understand.

"You don't have to see him if you don't want to. I can ask him to leave."

Jace said nothing. He was trying to think of what to do. He hadn't been prepared for this. He never thought Sheldon would actually show up when he wrote the letter. Instead, he was here. In person.

"Are you going to see him?"

"I don't think I have a choice," Jace said.

"I took him some food. He looks like he could use it."

Jace gave her a quick nod and turned. Slowly he walked to the door.

"Do you want me to go with you?" Kelly asked, stopping him.

He once more saw her in the brilliant sunlight. Shaking his head, he said, "I'll be all right."

Jace maneuvered through the crowds and

found Ari with the tour guide he'd befriended at the first open house.

Amy smiled at him. She was holding Ari's hand. "He's okay," she said. "He can stay with me."

Jace affectionately touched his son's head and moved around a group of visitors. He'd take the back stairway to avoid the rest of the craziness.

Grabbing a bottle of water from the kitchen, he walked up the back stairs. They opened onto a long, wide hallway that led to a master suite and six other bedrooms. On the next level were storage rooms where he used to hide and cry.

Jace didn't look at the steps to the third level. His eyes were fixed on the door to Sheldon's domain. The angle of light from the window behind him made Jace's shadow appear distorted over the maroon runner and the polished wooden floor. What was he going to say to his half brother? Why had Sheldon made the trip all the way here without any notice?

Jace moved toward the door. There was only one way he could find out. He was no longer the scared little boy. And he wouldn't be intimidated by a man who wouldn't give him a drink of water on a hot day. Remembering the bottle of water in his hand, Jace looked at it. Twisting the top off, he took a satisfying drink, replaced the screw cap and knocked on the door.

He didn't wait for an answer, but opened the door and went inside, closing it behind him. His brother was pacing the room, his back to Jace. Sheldon looked smaller, shorter than Jace remembered. Then he turned to face him.

And Jace saw the image of his father, stern and unforgiving.

CHAPTER EIGHTEEN

THE TWO BROTHERS faced each other like the Clantons faced the Earps at the OK Corral. Words weren't called for or necessary. Just draw and shoot, Jace thought. The only question was who would shoot first.

Sheldon's face was dark and craggy, as if he spent a lot of time in the sun. His hair was a mixture of grey and black, the black was still winning.

"How are you?" Sheldon finally asked. His voice was more raspy than Jace remembered, like a man who'd smoked all his life. But Sheldon didn't smoke.

Jace ignored the question. His half brother hadn't traveled four hundred miles to ask about his health.

"More important, why are you here?" Jace asked.

Sheldon cleared his throat and took a step forward. Jace looked at the table where the remnants of his meal sat. His brother stopped near it and lifted a glass of water. Setting it back on the table, he opened and closed his fists like a man who was nervous. Jace wondered what he had to be nervous about.

"I came to apologize," he said.

"Apologize," Jace repeated, feeling a little of the tension leave his body. "Apologize for what?"

"For being the person I was."

"Was? That indicates you've changed."

"I'm different," he said with a shake of his head. "I understand better now what I said and did to you, not what I should have done and not what you needed."

Sheldon could have written that in a note. He wanted to know what the real reason was for his coming here. Jace looked at his clothes. They were old and seemed as if he'd worn them for days. His shoes were dusty and he'd lost a lot of weight. Yet he was deeply tanned and appeared to be strong with toned muscles.

"Apology accepted. You can leave now." Jace turned to open the door, but was halted by a sound that was almost a wail.

"Wait!"

Jace turned back and looked at Sheldon. He wasn't lord of the manor anymore. Even his presence in this room, under which he used to command, he looked out of place, lost even.

"Could we sit down and talk?" His voice held a pleading quality Jace had never heard.

"Like all those brotherly talks we had in the past?" Sarcasm dripped from his lips, but it tasted sour.

"I know we never had any real talks—arguments, yes, but never talks. Not even when father died."

"Especially not then."

The reading of the will took place the day after their father was buried and everything went to Sheldon. Jace was only briefly mentioned—as if his existence meant nothing to his father. And Sheldon was smug and snobbish about the outcome.

"I want to tell you about my life," Sheldon said.

"Why would I be interested in that?"

"You might not, but I want to tell it to you anyway. I hope it will help you understand me and forgive me."

"That would have to be some life story," Jace spat.

Sheldon took a seat and crossed one leg over his knee. When Jace remained where he stood, his brother pushed a chair out and gestured for him to take it.

"Please," Sheldon said.

That was a word Jace could never remember hearing him utter, not even to the staff who made his life comfortable. Maybe he said it to Laura, but Jace hadn't stayed around long enough to find out.

Jace grabbed the chair and pulled it a little closer to the table. He set his water bottle in front of him and gave his attention to his half brother.

Sheldon again took a drink of water. He began with their father, telling Jace how he was raised, how the superior attitude he got had been drilled into him. He wanted to please the old man, so he did what he was told, spoke like he was expected to speak. When Jace came to live with them, their father was the only role model he had. He emulated him, did what he did, ridiculed and taunted because that's what he thought was expected.

"It never occurred to you to do anything else?" Jace interrupted.

"No," he answered. "You might have thought I should. I was a grown man and you were a child. But by then I'd been so conditioned to my own way of life that it felt right to do and say what I did. The fact that you were a terror in the county made it easier."

Jace looked away, taking a drink of his own water, before looking back at Sheldon. "So what's changed your mind?"

Sheldon pointed to the bedroom they were in. "This place." He looked back at his brother. "I ruined it."

Jace laughed. This was not the brother he knew. The self-righteous, never-wrong guy who tolerated no human frailties.

"It was my fault," Sheldon said. "I mismanaged the place. I had no idea how to run it well after father died. Laura helped for a while." He hung his head, was probably remembering his wife. "But alone, I was a poor excuse for looking after a farm this size or any size for that matter."

Jace listened to his brother pouring out his soul. He steeled himself to be wary, to not take what Sheldon said as truth. The man he'd grown up with probably had a hidden agenda.

Sheldon went on, telling him how he'd lived after leaving the Kendall, moving from state to state, trying to get work on another farm and how people turned him down or fired him after a short stay. He told Jace he'd been homeless, that he'd sifted through garbage cans looking for food.

Jace listened silently, forcing away any sympathy he had as unworthy of this man who looked so much like thier implacable father.

"Then, when I was in North Carolina, I met a guy who knew of a job," Sheldon said. "I went to ask about it and I got it. I clean barnacles off the hulls of pleasure boats."

Jace wasn't sure he'd heard right. "You do what?"

"I take care of boats at a marina. Repair and repaint them if needed."

Jace opened his mouth, but said nothing.

"I know. It's menial work," Sheldon said. "I live in a bungalow on the beach and I read a lot of library books."

Jace's eyes must have betrayed his feelings.

"Don't feel sorry for me. I'm happy, probably for the first time in my life. Oh, I was happy with Laura, more so than I ever thought I would be, but we were caught up in material things, thought nothing could touch us. Not until she died and I moved away did I understand what both joy and sadness could be."

"And you came to tell me this?"

Sheldon nodded. "Audrey, she's a friend in North Carolina, teaches kindergarten, it was her suggestion that I contact you."

"What do you want me to do?"

"Nothing," he said. "You're the main reason I came, but there is another one. It's for me. I couldn't go on living with the way I had treated you."

"So you're absolved now?" Jason asked, leaning forward in his chair. "A four-hundred-mile trip and a few words negate the years of abuse I took from you and dad?"

Sheldon was shaking his head. "Nothing will absolve that. From me or from father. Neither you nor I can change it. What we can do is choose to understand it. Or not."

"Suppose I choose not?" Jace asked.

"That's your right. I hope you don't. I'd

like us to be friends or at least stay in touch with each other. But if that isn't possible, I will, of course, accept that. Most of what happened to you was my fault. I'm willing to take the blame."

"You're going to play the martyr." Jace chuckled. "That is what you do. You rode around on your horse as if you were king of all you surveyed."

"And you raced through the countryside on horseback or in a car terrorizing all who came in contact with you." Sheldon stopped and took a long breath. "I apologize. I'm not here to resurrect old wounds. I only wanted to tell you I'm sorry."

Sheldon stood up. "I'll leave now. It was good to see you. Ms. Ashton tells me you have a son. Congratulations."

Emotions Jace had never known warred inside him. He watched his half brother head for the door. Why should he feel anything but contempt for him? Yet he felt sorry. He wanted to believe Sheldon. He'd always wanted him to change, to accept him. Now it seemed he was offering friendship and Jace was rejecting it. What should he do? What would Kelly think?

Sheldon had his hand on the doorknob when Jace asked, "Do you want to meet him?"

"THE CHANDELIER WAS brought over from Europe during the Victorian period," Amy, the tour guide, spoke to her group as they looked up at the ballroom ceiling. "It's made of both straight and a rare curved crystal."

As soon as Ari saw Jace, he abandoned the tour guide and rushed to his father. Amy looked up and recognized his brother. Jace smiled and she nodded.

"Ladies and gentlemen, this is a rare pleasure." Amy turned and opened her arm to include the newcomers to the group. "This is Mr. Sheldon Kendall, the former owner of Kendall Farm."

Jace heard the intake of breath from the group when Sheldon was introduced. "And this is my brother, Jason Kendall," he said. The fact that Sheldon introduced him as his brother wasn't lost on Jace. He'd always referred to Sheldon as his half brother.

"Do you guide any of the tours?" a woman in the audience asked.

Sheldon answered before Jace could say

anything. "No, ma'am. I live in North Carolina now."

Jace wondered if Sheldon was saving him
from an awkward moment. Their talk earlier
had alleviated some of their hostility. Jace no
longer hated his brother, but he didn't love
him either, not with the unconditional love
that families should have for one another. But
a lot of the weight on his shoulders seemed
to be gone.

"Go on with the tour," Jace said. "We'll
take Ari." Cupping the boy's hand, the two
men walked away from the group.

Jace led Ari through the kitchen where he
picked up a small bottle of orange juice and
a straw. He handed it to the boy. Then they
went out on the back porch. He sat down on
a wicker sofa and pulled Ari against him. Ari
opened the orange juice and drank. Sheldon
sat across from them.

"Ari, this is Sheldon," Jace began.

Ari looked like a child who didn't know if
he was in trouble or not.

"He's your uncle."

"Uncle." Ari smiled. "I have an uncle." He
studied Sheldon carefully, holding the bottle

of orange juice close to him. "How do I get an uncle?"

"I'm your father's brother," Sheldon said. He kept his eyes on the boy and didn't meet Jace's gaze. Jace thought that was the second time he'd ever referred to him as his brother and not his half brother.

Ari looked at Jace. "You have a brother?"

Jace nodded.

"Wow. Can I have one?"

Both men laughed.

"You live in the North," Ari told Sheldon. "How can you be my uncle?"

Sheldon shifted in his chair so that he and the four-year-old were close to the same level.

"I live in North Carolina, not the North," Sheldon clarified. "It's near the ocean."

"Wow, can you swim in it?"

Sheldon looked amused. "Of course you can."

"Ari, Sheldon is my brother. He used to live here at the Kendall. That's how he's your uncle."

"Do you have children?" Ari asked, swinging his attention to Sheldon.

Sheldon shook his head. "No, we never had children."

Jace knew he was thinking of Laura again. He wondered why the two had not had children. He knew Laura wanted them. She had a couple of sisters who were married and she had wanted a family, too. Jace was unsure what his brother thought about children. Sheldon had never shared those thoughts with him. Sheldon had rarely shared anything with him.

"Oh," Ari looked down as if he was disappointed.

"But…" Sheldon offered him hope. "I have a friend named Christian. He's older than you are. He's nine."

"I'm going to be nine," Ari stated.

"You're going to be five," Jace corrected.

"I'm sure Christian would love to meet you. He hasn't been around any horses. Maybe you could show him how to ride."

Ari's face lit up. He twisted around and looked at Jace, his top lip coated with orange juice. "Can I, Dad?"

"I think so," Jace said.

Jace looked at his brother. He was unsure if this was real or a trick. If it was a trick, Sheldon was good, since Jace was falling for his lines. Sheldon had apologized and was ready to walk out the door only hours after he'd arrived. He said nothing about where he was staying or how long he would be in Maryland. Jace wasn't sure of a lot things, but for now he'd wait and see.

"Can we go get him today?" Ari asked with enthusiasm.

"He lives a long way from here, Ari," Jace said.

"Can we go tomorrow?"

Jace smiled at him.

Sheldon spoke up. "I'd like it if you would come to see me. I live in a small bungalow with only one bedroom, but I'm sure we could rough it for a few days. It's right on the beach and there's an arcade close by."

"What's an arc...arc...?"

"Arcade," Sheldon supplied. "It's a place with a lot of games that kids like to play."

"Video games?" Ari's eyes opened wide. Video games were heaven to him.

Sheldon nodded. "Christian loves video games. He's got a lot of them at his house. I'm sure he'd let you play with them."

"Wow," Ari said.

THE ORANGE JUICE bottle was emptied with a loud gurgle. Ari went inside to recycle the plastic bottle. He ran back to the door and swung it open.

"Dad, can we ride the horses?"

"Not on visitors' day," Jace repeated the rule he'd established during their first open house.

"Okay, I'm going to find Kelly," he announced and tore away before Jace could say anything. "I want to tell her about the arcade."

"Is he always that fast?" Sheldon asked.

Jace nodded.

"You must be very proud," Sheldon said. He stood up then and went to the edge of the porch.

"I am," Jace said, joining him. Jace walked down the steps and across the path that led to the stables. His brother followed.

"Where's his mother?" Sheldon asked.

"Dead," Jace replied.

"I'm sorry. I suppose we've both lost a wife."

"We were never married," Jace said without further explanation. He'd let Sheldon think what he would.

They reached the stables and took a moment to look in on the horses. "Only two," Sheldon said.

"For the time being. There'll be more," Jace told him.

"I suppose it takes time to get everything back to the way it was," Sheldon said.

Jace agreed, but said nothing. He went beyond the stables to the fence that lined the property.

"Tell me about Laura," Jace said. So far no one had told him the entire story of what had happened to her.

"Laura died four years ago," he said. "Jace, I didn't mean to steal her—"

"Don't." Jace put his hand up so his brother wouldn't continue. "Don't apologize. As long as we're saying things we should have said ages ago, I want you to know I no longer hold it against you for marrying Laura. I know now that I liked Laura, liked her a lot, but I wasn't really in love with her." He knew what he felt for Kelly was much stronger than anything he'd felt for Laura.

"When I saw you two together, your love shone so bright, even I could see it. But I was so angry with you for the years of hurt, that Laura was just the final straw."

"Thanks for that," Sheldon said. "It's weighed heavily on my mind for years." Jace turned toward Sheldon. "Where did you go?" Sheldon asked. "After the wedding? After you left here."

"I don't remember a lot of it," Jace said. "I bummed around, drank. I was in Germany and Italy for a while."

Sheldon glanced at him.

"I surfaced in Greece, dirty and out of money. Then I signed on to a freighter and ended up in South America. In Colombia I got a job as an engineer for a water company. I stayed for three years."

"Why did you come back?"

"The Kendall is my home." Jace stated it matter of factly, without emotion. "And Ari needed better medical care. We returned a couple of months ago. Kelly took us in and gave me a job."

"She told me you were no longer here."

"I'm not. The job ended." Jace was embarrassed to admit why he'd been asked to go.

"Is Ari very ill? He doesn't look it."

"He's not ill at all. The diagnosis in Colombia was incorrect. He had some allergies, but he's a healthy boy and he loves horses."

Sheldon smiled. Jace realized that was probably the first smile he could ever remember on his brother's face, except where Laura was concerned.

"How long were you with Ari's mother?"

It appeared his brother was trying to make up for the years they hadn't been in touch, in a short space of time.

"Never was. Ari is not my biological child. I adopted him. His mother died in an explosion. She saved Ari by throwing him to me. I couldn't find any relatives of the boy, so I adopted him."

Again Sheldon smiled and nodded. Jace had the feeling his half brother was approving of his actions. This was new. Sheldon differed with all his decisions, even if it was just to be contrary. Time had changed more than his appearance. He was a different man inside and out.

"So, how did she die?" Jace asked, returning to the story of Laura.

"Breast cancer. She had surgery, chemo, radiation, but in the end nothing could save her. Her last days were awful, she was in so much pain, the morphine offered only some respite." Jace could see Sheldon was struggling with telling the story. Even now his brother loved Laura. "When Laura died, I lost all interest in doing anything."

Sheldon's voice was full of sorrow.

"I wasn't a good manager of the Kendall anyway. I'd never been good at it."

Jace remembered the books he'd seen and how the Kendall had been losing money for years.

"While Laura was here, she was the one who kept things on track. She was the better manager. But after her death, everything went to ruin." He took a moment to glance at the barn. "But it appears Ms. Ashton has put a lot of the glory back in the house and grounds."

"She's trying to make the place self-sustaining. That's why there are so many people in the house today. She opens it to the public once a week, collecting fees to pay for upkeep. I was against it at first, but I realize it couldn't be done without some sort of compromise, and Kelly is doing a great job."

"It's good to see it like this. When I left it was practically falling apart. I'm amazed at what she's accomplished."

Jace scanned the area, too. There was a

lot that was different now. But it was good different.

He knew some of Kelly's plans for the future. He had hoped maybe he and Ari could be a part of them, but that was no longer on the cards.

KELLY HAD TOO much going on with the open house to worry about what was happening between Jace and Sheldon. Yet she couldn't concentrate on anything else. One of the guides had a mishap, though, and Kelly had to take on leading his tour group.

Throughout the day she'd handled question after question about everything from the china and wall coverings, to when the house had central heating installed—the answer to that one, the 1920s.

She was relieved when five o'clock arrived and the last guests left the gift shop and returned to the parking lot.

Curious to know how the conversation between Jace and Sheldon was going, she went in search of the two brothers. It wasn't long before Kelly heard male voices on the back porch. She couldn't help herself, she went to the kitchen and gathered a tray and added iced tea, a couple of sandwiches and several tea cakes that were becoming a specialty of the Kendall. At the screen door, she listened for any sign that Jace and Sheldon might be arguing. Instead of a fight, she could hear laughing. Balancing the tray with one hand, she pressed on the door and stepped outside.

Jace twisted around in his chair and looked at her. Immediately, he was on his feet and coming forward to take the tray. Sheldon made room on the table at which they were sitting and Jace placed it there.

"You've been here so long, I thought you both might need some food." She tested the atmosphere for tension and found it only slightly charged. She tried to figure out what was going on. Were they agreeing to a plan for the Kendall?

Kelly had a sip of her iced tea. "Jace, I hope it's all right, I told Ari we could go for a ride before dinner."

"Dinner?" Jace checked his watch. "I didn't realize it was so late."

"You're all welcome to stay." She included both men in her gaze and they nodded. It was the hospitable thing to do, but that wasn't the only reason Kelly invited them. She missed seeing Ari and Jace. And she wanted to know what the brothers were discussing and what Jace was going to do about the Kendall's sale.

Now that the Kendalls were reunited, however precariously, they could pose a united front and push her out. They'd been together for more than two hours. What had they talked about? Was any of their discussion related to the Kendall and wrestling it back due to a technicality in the paperwork?

Kelly was determined to find out.

CHAPTER NINETEEN

THE FORMAL DINING room had a table and chairs to serve twenty. With only five of them for dinner, it was much too large for tonight's meal. Rather, a smaller and more intimate room lay off the kitchen. It looked out on the western side of the house, across the porch and into the far woods. The sun had not yet set, but it was on its way down. Flowers had been added to the room, giving it a subtle fragrance. Kelly placed folded napkins and china on the table. She used the good silver and crystal glasses.

The members assembled, a little awkwardly, and took seats. Ari had eaten earlier and was playing video games on a handheld device.

"Sheldon, why don't you sit there instead?" She pointed to a seat opposite the one Jace was standing behind. She sat next to Jace.

Kelly hoped they'd be able to break the

ice at dinner. She had a purpose for wanting to speak with the brothers. She wondered if they had an offer to present to her. Drew and Mira were there for moral support.

"Sheldon, did you have time to see the house?" Drew began. "Kelly has done a wonderful job restoring it."

Sheldon smiled at her. She thought how opposite the two brothers looked, even with different mothers. "Jace took me on a tour before dinner. Kelly, you've done a lot."

She nodded toward him, acknowledging his sincere words. "I found some old photographs of the rooms and used them as a basis for some of the restoration."

Earlier, she'd offered a member of the kitchen staff extra wages if she'd prepare a simple dinner for the group. Fortunately, Grace had agreed, and they now began to pass the serving dishes around the table. The main meal consisted of a salad, seared fish with fresh asparagus and glazed sweet potatoes. Sheldon refused the wine, but accepted a glass of water.

Kelly took the opportunity to switch subjects. "How do you like living in North Carolina?"

"It's warmer. We rarely get snow and the sunsets are amazing."

"What do you do there?" Mira asked.

"I work at a boat yard. I clean the hulls. Do repairs."

"Do you plan to stay there, settle for the long run?" Kelly asked. It was the perfect opening for her to find out his agenda. Why had he shown up at the Kendall out of the blue?

"I think so," he said.

She nearly closed her eyes in relief.

"I have a job. I don't plan to keep it for the rest of my life."

"What do you plan to do?" Mira asked.

"I'm thinking of becoming an electrician." He went on to explain his reasons and that he'd already begun to learn about it.

"I'm glad to hear that," Jace said. "I know it's hard to change from one thing to another. I'm about to do the same thing."

Kelly's fork clattered onto her plate. All eyes went to Jace.

"I got a job today," he said.

"Job?" Kelly questioned.

He nodded. "That's the reason for the suit." He leaned back in his chair.

The room was deathly quiet. Yes, Kelly had thrown him off the farm, but in the back of her mind, she thought he'd come back. If he didn't challenge her for ownership, then she thought they would resolve their differences, but if he had a job...

"Where?" she asked.

"County land office. I'm the new engineer for Duchess County. Sort of like a surveyor. I enrolled Ari in that day-care center, which he loves, and I'll be looking for a permanent place for us to live."

"That's a lot of change," Mira said.

"It is, but we can't live here. And my savings aren't going to let us continue to live at the motel."

He was in a motel. Kelly felt like a louse. How could she throw him and his son out with no place to live? She felt her face grow hot.

"Maybe Kelly will let you come back until you find somewhere else," Sheldon said. "This is a big house. I'm sure you two can get around without bumping into each other."

All the eyes that had been on Jace were now on her. They silently asked for a response.

"Of course," she said. What else could she

say. "We have the horses and Ari loves riding them. I don't imagine it will take long to find a nice place. Not in this market."

"We'll talk about it later," Jace said. He must have heard the reluctance in her voice.

"Staying here until then sounds perfect," Mira stated. "Ari can still go to the day-care center and he'll have this treat to come home to until you get off work. I'm sure that job could send you away at times."

She looked at Kelly. "And you love having him around."

Kelly glared at her cousin. She felt like the walls were closing in, yet there was nothing she could do to stop them. Even her own family wasn't standing up for her. Mira was throwing her into the lion's den.

And they both knew why.

As dinner ended and the dishes were being moved to the kitchen, Jace stopped Kelly. Angling her onto the porch, he leaned with his back to the railing. Kelly faced him.

"I'm not going to stay here," he told her.

She took a breath before asking, "Why?"

"Ari and I need to be settled." She thought they could settle here, but didn't say it. She'd become used to having them around.

"What about the Kendall?" she asked.

"The Kendall is yours."

Kelly blinked, unsure she'd heard the words she so wanted to hear.

"Sheldon is returning to North Carolina," Jace said. "Ari and I will find a small place. He'll go to school and I'll work. The Kendall is yours."

Kelly felt numb. She moved to one of the rocking chairs and sat on the edge of it.

"You're not going to challenge me on it?" Jace smiled and shook his head.

"What changed your mind?" she asked.

"I realized it's just a house. In Colombia, our apartment was small, but we were happy. We don't need the Kendall for that. Now that I have a job and day care for Ari, we need to get on with our lives. We should have done this when we first arrived."

Kelly thought of the Kendall without them and her heart lurched. She was getting what she wanted. So why didn't she feel like she'd won?

SHELDON STAYED FOR four days, enjoying the hospitality of Kelly and the Kendall. Consequently, Jace was also underfoot. Kelly couldn't turn a corner without seeing one or the other of the brothers. Ari was also by her side. He enjoyed day care, but couldn't wait to get to the horses when it was home time.

Sheldon left on a Saturday. Ari said good-bye and hugged his uncle. It was a moment that Jace seemed to appreciate given his wide smile. Then she and Ari mounted a horse and went for a ride while Jace took his brother to the bus station. She and Ari rode longer and farther than ever before. Ari sat in front of her. She took him to the place where she grew up. It was about a mile beyond the Kendall's south border. Her house was still there, although it was occupied by another family. The neighborhood had changed. When she lived here it was poor and run-down. Since then new families had moved in and fixed everything up.

Slipping down from the saddle, Kelly reached up and helped Ari to the ground. She tied the horse to a nearby tree at the edge of the neighborhood.

"Where are we?" Ari asked.

"This is where I used to live," she told him. "I thought you might like to see it."

She sat down on the curb and pulled Ari onto her knee.

Ari looked around. "Which house was yours?"

"The yellow one over there." Kelly pointed to a small, neat house with a bay window and a black door.

"Who lives there now?"

"Some other people."

"Don't you want to live there?"

"I live at the Kendall. I like living there."

"Can I live at the Kendall, too?" he asked.

Kelly wasn't sure how to answer that. She'd love for Ari to live there, but that was impossible. "Don't you want to live with your dad?"

"Yeah. I want him to live at the Kendall, too. It's got our name. Does that mean it belongs to us?"

She repositioned him closer to her. "It's not that easy. It does have your name, but it was sold and someone else owns it now."

"You own it?" he asked.

"Yeah," she said, using his word.

"We used to stay with you. Can't we do it again?"

"That's a very hard question, too. You see, your dad worked for me when you lived there.

But he has another job now. It's closer to your day care. And next September you'll be going to school."

"We can't do all that and still live at the Kendall?" His voice was straining and Kelly knew he would start to cry soon. She wanted to cry, too. She wanted them back, both of them. But things were complicated. How could she ever trust Jace again?

Kelly stared at her old house again. In the front yard was a pink bicycle. The owners must have a daughter. Kelly wasn't sure she'd have a family of her own and it seemed less likely now. She loved Jace, but she couldn't see it working out between them.

"Come on, Ari. Let's go back."

The two mounted the mare and Kelly led it into a slow walk. After a while they were back at the fence and heading for the Kendall.

"Dad!" Ari called as Jace came into view. Kelly stopped the horse and helped Ari get down safely. He took off in a dead run for Jace. She watched the scene as father and son greeted each other. Then she turned the mare toward the stable. Inside she began the procedure of rubbing the horse down. She didn't really need it. They hadn't ridden the horse hard. It didn't even break a sweat. But Kelly wanted to give Jace time to collect Ari and leave the Kendall.

She took more time than necessary. When she came out of the stable Jace and Ari were no longer where she'd left them. She didn't see them anywhere. Kelly was both relieved and disappointed. It was nearly dinnertime, but she wasn't hungry. She thought she'd go for a drive. She hadn't been out of the Kendall in weeks except to run errands for the estate.

As she entered through the back door to get her car keys and purse, Jace came in and met her. "Oh, hi," she said. "I thought you and Ari were gone."

"Ari's watching something on television. I wanted to talk to you."

This was it, Kelly thought. "Why don't we go—"

"For a walk," he finished for her.

"What about Ari?" she protested. She didn't want to be alone with Jace. It was far too dangerous. Her feelings were too strong and he was supposed to be her enemy. It was getting dark. And while Ari was a poor substitute for a chaperone, he was all she had.

Jace took her hand and led her out the front door. "We're only going to circle around the house. Ari knows where we are and we'll also be within shouting distance if he needs us."

"Did Sheldon get away all right?" Kelly asked, going down the steps.

"He did. He liked his visit, but said he was looking forward to going back to North Carolina."

"He seemed different from how you described him."

Jace pulled her arm through his. Kelly resisted a little, but didn't fight him.

"He's different from what I remember, too. Seems he's changed and for the better. Kind of surreal, acutally."

"How do you mean?" she asked.

"His manner was calm, accepting, way less confrontational than it used to be. When I first saw him again, I was prepared for him to berate me for some offense. Instead, he apologized."

"So you two mended fences."

"Not totally. Have to admit I kept waiting for the real Sheldon to show up. I figured he had an ulterior motive and I was trying to figure out what it was."

"But," she prompted.

"If he had one, he must have changed his mind about it. All the way until the bus left the station, he apologized for all the things he'd done to me when we lived here."

"That must have made you feel good."

"It did. He invited us to visit him in North Carolina. Ari is excited about going to the ocean."

"You should go," Kelly said. "I'm sure Ari would love the water. And you could get to know your brother better." She glanced at him. "Assuming you want to know him better."

Kelly was an only child. She had a score of cousins, but no siblings. She hadn't grown up with anyone in the house but her parents. She knew they loved her, even her father after her mother's death and he began to drink, he still loved her. She'd never had anyone tearing her down, ripping away at her self-esteem as Jace had.

"People do change, Jace. When he talked to me, he seemed genuine. At dinner he didn't try to hide anything."

"I know and that impressed me even more." Jace stopped walking and turned to her. The sun had set and it was dark. "He asked about you."

"Me? What did he want to know?"

"How things were between us. I wasn't sure what to say."

Kelly stiffened.

"He thinks you've done a terrific job with the house and grounds. He was proud of the place and glad it was being taken care of with so much love."

Kelly smiled. "Thank you. I'm glad about that."

"I know it's a labor of love for you. I think Sheldon saw that, too."

That should have made Kelly feel good, but it had the opposite effect. She felt guilty.

"Jace, I haven't had a chance to apologize for how we ended things. I'm—"

"You were right from the start, Kelly. I should never have gone behind your back. It was deceitful and I should be the one apologizing. I'm sorry."

"That means a lot to me, Jace. Thanks. I'm glad things are working out for you. The engineering job must take a lot off your mind."

"It does. Ari likes going to the day-care center. You should have seen him when he discovered all those toys and the other kids. In a few months he'll be in kindergarten." Jace paused. His eyes traveled over her face. "He misses you," Jace said, his voice ragged as if it hurt to say the words.

"I…" Kelly stopped. She couldn't say anything. Jace was gazing at her with so much tenderness in his eyes that it robbed Kelly of her ability to speak. She couldn't drag her gaze away, either.

"Thank you," Jace said.

"For what?" she asked.

"For the past few days. For opening the Kendall to Sheldon. For sending Emmett to find me. For being you."

Kelly frowned, embarrassed at the flood of compliments. "I need to thank you, too, for something else."

"For what?"

"The horses. For the contract you negotiated. For helping out with the Kendall despite how you feel—"

He stopped her, lifted her chin until she was looking into his eyes. Kelly was unable to move, unable to pull away from him. Jace leaned in and kissed her. Her heart pounded, pumping through her body with a force so hard it scared her. His mouth descended on hers, soft and warm. As he folded her into his arms, she knew she was safe and that she wanted to stay there forever.

Jace raised his head and Kelly wrangled out of his arms. She was breathless. The stars were out and a full moon shone overhead. She knew it had been dangerous to walk in the moonlight. Now he'd kissed her and Kelly was more rattled than ever.

Her eyes were full of unshed tears. "I think you should go now," she said.

"Kelly, I'm sorry. I didn't mean to—"

He hadn't meant to kiss her. He hadn't meant to confuse her. He hadn't meant to have her fall in love with him. It was too late. All those things had happened. If she was going to survive his presence and the Kendall, she had to remain in control. And he'd just proven that with him, she had none. Jace removed his hands and stepped back. Kelly remained where she was, but the urge to run was so strong she had to dig her fingers into her palms to stay in place. Jace gave her a long look. She couldn't interpret it in the dim light. They both stood like wavering branches that only needed a small wind to push them together. She knew if that wind came she would be lost.

Kelly stepped farther away. The movement seemed to cut the invisible connection holding them together. Jace went up the seven steps and opened the door. Kelly heard him call Ari's name as he went inside. She wouldn't wait for them to come out. She wouldn't wait for them to say goodbye. She didn't know when she would see Ari again. He had a routine to follow. And so did she. The sooner they fell into step, the better for all, Kelly thought.

But Jace had kissed her again. He knew how she felt. It had been in the kiss.

WOULD LIFE EVER return to normal? Kelly asked herself that question, uncertain what her next move would be. Rain had come again. The huge swings in summer temperatures made for thunderstorms and evening downpours. Often they didn't last long.

The rain slowed. Kelly went out on the front porch. The temperature dropped and the rain seemed to have washed everything clean. The air felt fresh. Kelly loved that smell. She walked the length of the porch and looked out over the grounds. She listened for the horses, making sure their sounds were normal.

Sheldon had been unlike what Kelly was expecting. He was humble, apologetic and appeared to want Jace's forgiveness.

Forgiveness...

Kelly paced slowly, methodically. She'd worked so long and hard on the Kendall, she'd lost sight of the fact that it was only a house. Jace had said that. And now she felt it, too. It was huge, but without the life that Jace and Ari brought to it.

Kelly shuddered as a gust of wind forced the rain to shower her. It was cold and reflected her feelings. While the building had once been warm and inviting, she felt it was cold and lonely now. It needed Jace.

He'd walked away as if he could go on without being here, but Kelly knew he loved the Kendall more now than when he first arrived. And he was sacrificing it for her.

She didn't need or want his sacrifice. She liked the glory of working on the house, restoring it to its former beauty, but she didn't want to stay here with the memories of a family and not have that family.

There was New York, she thought. She

could go back there. She'd have a huge salary, a staff of her own, big-money accounts. And *Perry*. She frowned. He was a big disadvantage, but she could handle him. Returning to New York wouldn't be so bad. She'd have less renovations to worry about. She'd be able to afford a loft and could decorate it the way she wanted.

She'd miss seeing the land and especially this horizon. She'd miss this smell after the rain. She'd miss the horses. She'd also miss Jace and Ari. But being hours away from them would make it easier for her to get over thinking about Jace and what he'd done to her. She should hate him, but she couldn't. How could she hate a man she'd fallen in love with?

IT WAS THE evening of the day after he left Maryland, when Sheldon stepped down from the bus and looked around. He was back in Meadesville. The air smelled like salt and gulls. The sky was turning a deep blue in preparation for nightfall. He took a deep breath, inhaling the familiar scents he'd become used to in the past year. It was good to be back. That world at the Kendall was no longer his. He was grateful that Audrey had talked him into going. Now he knew what he was leaving behind and he had no regrets about the house and the land. It was in good hands and he was proud to have his name on it. Proud that his brother and his nephew would be there, at least in town, and close to the their old home. He wished it was Jason's property, but he realized that Kelly loved the place just as much as a Kendall by birth.

Here in North Carolina Sheldon felt he had a real purpose. He'd never have learned that if he was still running the Kendall and failing at it. He was going to take a course to be an electrician, for which he'd receive financial aid. The man Audrey had introduced him to told him about the course. When he completed the classes, Sheldon would sign on as an apprentice with Audrey's friend. At the Kendall, Sheldon would turn on a light and walk into a room without a second thought. Once he completed his course, he'd know exactly how to fix the electricity instead. Hopefully, his apprenticeship would lead to a full-time job.

Meanwhile, the bungalow was all the space he needed for now. And he liked having Audrey and Christian as friends. He didn't know where his relationship with Audrey was going, but as time passed, they would find out. Where were Audrey and Christian? He'd called to say he was coming back today.

Sheldon headed toward the small building that served as the bus station. Christian came running through the door before Sheldon got to it.

"Sheldon! You're back." Christian launched himself at Sheldon. They hugged. Sheldon knew how Jace felt about his son. He felt a similar way about Christian. Seeing the boy made his heart swell.

Audrey came up behind her grandson. Sheldon was happy to have someone to come home to. Someone who cared about him.

"Hello," she said.

Sheldon leaned down and kissed her cheek. He thought of Jason and Kelly, wondering how long it would take his brother to figure out that he was in love with her.

"Thanks for coming," Sheldon said.

The three piled into her car. During the drive, she passed the marina and his bungalow and drove to her house. "You had a long trip," she said. "I thought you might be hungry."

"I'm starving," he told her.

"Me, too," Christian said from the backseat. "Grandma made something with a fancy name, but it's really just chicken and rice."

"Arroz con pollo," Audrey supplied.

"I'd love that," Sheldon said.

He should be tired. It was a twenty-four-hour bus ride with stops everywhere and a layover in Washington, DC. But seeing Audrey and Christian rejuvenated him. They had dinner while Christian grilled him on every aspect of his trip. The three sat at the table long after the meal was over.

Moving to the porch, they looked out at the ocean until Christian went to bed. Audrey went in with him but soon returned. She sat down, handing Sheldon a glass of ice water. She had a cup of tea.

"So, how was it really?" she began.

"Better than I expected. Jason and I had a long talk. We're not friends, but we're no longer enemies."

She smiled into her cup. It was her way of not saying I told you so. "What about the woman who owns the farm? Kelly, right?"

"Right. I like her. She's doing everything she can to make the place work. You should see some of the things she'd done. I'd never have thought of those changes. And all of them are within the original architecture of the house."

Audrey smiled.

"What?"

"Your voice is excited, proud even, when you talk about the house. Are you sure leaving it behind is what you want?"

"I'm sure."

"What about your brother?"

Sheldon sighed. Jason had told him about the lawyer he'd hired to look into the sale and the possibility of reversing it due to a technicality in the wording of the contract, but Sheldon thought it wouldn't make sense to do so. Jason had a job and could support his son. He hadn't really ever lived at the Kendall. Giving it up should be easier for him, but Sheldon didn't think so.

"I'm not sure about Jason. He's in love with Kelly, but I don't think either of them knows it." He took a drink of water. "There is one thing, though."

"What's that?"

"Kelly is putting all her love into making the Kendall a grand mansion and horse farm. I have no doubt that it'll succeed."

"So are you going back there again? To see your brother or his son?"

"I hope so. But only for a visit. My home is here now."

KELLY WASN'T SLEEPING WELL. She was tired as soon as she got out of bed in the morning. Jace and Sheldon were weighing heavy on her mind. Eventually, she dressed and got a cup of coffee. She had a wedding scheduled for tomorrow and the Kendall would be over-run with service people and vendors delivering everything from the cake to flowers to dinner place cards. Kelly had worked with the wedding consultant. She wasn't nearly as efficient as the first one. Consequently, Kelly had a lot more details to see to and she needed to be at her best.

Finishing her cup of coffee, she poured a second one and went to her office. The phone was ringing. She didn't really want to answer it this early, but she had no choice.

"Kendall Farm, this is Kelly Ashton."

"Kelly... Perry here."

Perry. She'd forgotten about him and that she was supposed to be thinking over his offer.

Clearing her throat, she said, "Perry, wasn't I supposed to call you?"

"I had a talk with Grissom yesterday. They're eager to get to work with you. I thought I'd see when we could expect you. Your office has been painted and decorated, but if there's anything you don't like, you have carte blanche to change it."

He was truly sweetening the pot. Why shouldn't she tell him she'd be right there? Unconsciously, Kelly opened her calendar.

"Perry, I have several contracts that will have to be fulfilled."

"I understand," he said. "If necessary, we can split your time until they are completed."

He really must need her badly, if he was willing to make this many concessions.

"Perry," she said. "How about..." She scrolled down a few weeks. Her calendar was covered with events for the Kendall. None of them mattered. Kelly knew it would be short notice to cancel them, but it could be done.

"Are you still there?" Perry asked.

"I'm checking my dates," she said. "How about next month. Say the…"

"Say no."

Kelly froze. The voice came from the doorway. She knew Jace's voice. She could pick it out anywhere.

"Say no," he said again. "Don't leave."

Kelly held the phone away from her ear. Jace came into the room.

"Stay," he said. "The Kendall is part of you. You'll do a good job in New York, but you'll never love it the way you love this place."

"I can't stay here alone."

"This is your home," Jace said. "It's where you belong. Where we all belong. You took this place and gave it life. It's what I wanted it to be. I wanted it full of love when I was a boy. And that's what I want for Ari. For us. You've done that for us all. Don't give up. Say no."

"I thought you didn't want to stay here. You and Ari were going to find—"

"I thought about it and realized anywhere is good if you're with me, but nowhere will be perfect without you."

Kelly's heart pounded in her chest. "I love

you, Kelly Ashton. I want you to be my wife." He took another step closer to her and went down on one knee. "Will you marry me? Will you take me and my son and will you allow the three of us to make this a real home?"

Kelly stared at Jace. Everything she wanted in the world lay at her feet. She dropped the phone and fell into Jace's arms.

"Yes," she said, tears falling freely. "I love you, too. Yes. Yes. Yes," she cried. "I'll marry you."

Jace pulled her out of the chair and onto his knee. He kissed her, a long, slow tender kiss that she'd never forget. There was no stopping this time. And Kelly didn't push him away. She didn't tell him not to confuse her. She wanted to be confused. She wanted to be everything to him.

She was happier than anyone. This was her future. Jace was her prince. And they would build together. They would make the Kendall the showplace it was always intended to be. But more than that, they would make it a home. And they would do it with love.

EPILOGUE

Three Years Later

JACE STOOD ON the track. He held the bridle of the horse. Ari sat in the saddle. The boy had grown into a tall, gangly seven-year-old. He took to a horse as if the two of them spoke the same language. This was to be Ari's inaugural ride, his solo.

Kelly sat in the stands watching. She'd done what she set out to do. She'd gotten the race track and stadium built. She'd been through countless council meetings, building inspections, gaming license reviews, water and sewer testing, new road construction and a thousand more things. Yet she got all the permits, all the approvals, and finally the track had become a reality. It was scheduled to open tomorrow.

Oh, and she'd had their two babies.

She'd even helped to mend things between

him and his brother. After Sheldon got his electrician's license, she'd hired the firm he worked for, transporting them to the Kendall, to do the wiring on the track. With the income derived from the marketing programs she had in place, and a substantial investment from the bank, they'd spared no expense on the setup.

The stables were full of horses that practiced daily on the new track and were ready to race. The vendors had brought in inventory and stocked their shelves. Ticket sellers had been hired. Television commercials had been running on cable for over a month. Everything was in place.

Jace glanced at his wife. She was a marvel. He couldn't believe his luck. Beside Kelly were Drew and Mira. Jace regarded them as his cousins, too. He no longer distinguished between bloodlines. He knew there was more to family than that. Mira held her and Drew's two-year-old son.

Sheldon, Audrey and Christian still lived in North Carolina, but they'd be arriving in time for the opening of the racetrack.

Jace's two new additions smiled at him as they kicked the seats in front of them. His daughter, Meghan, was two. His one-year-old son, Jason, couldn't quite reach the seat, but he tried, emulating his sister. They were all there to see Ari make his first trip around the track.

Jace was slightly apprehensive. Ari was still young, though an excellent horseman. The track was a mile around and Jace would be holding his breath for every second of Ari's ride. From the look on Kelly's face, she would be, too.

"Remember, Ari, this is not a race. Take it easy," he warned.

"I *know*, dad," Ari said. His tone told Jace he'd heard that same message enough times.

"Okay, just be careful." Jace stepped back. "He's all yours."

Ari kicked his feet and the horse began to walk. Leaning down, Ari's expression said he was serious about controlling the powerful animal. Jace watched until Ari completed the entire mile track. Ari came back at a gallop, passing his father and all those in the stands. Jace had spotted a huge grin on his face as horse and rider sped by.

Ari reined the horse in, bringing him to a slow trot and then walking him back to Jace.

Everyone cheered. Ari smiled. Drew snapped a photo to capture the moment.

"Did you see me, Dad?" Ari asked, excited and out of breath. "Did you see me?"

"You were wonderful," Jace told him.

As Drew and Mira came forward to congratulate Ari, Jace took the bridle and looped the horse's reins over the fencing. He then put his arm around Kelly.

Finally Jace had everything he ever wanted— a family he adored and one that adored him. The Kendall had been restored and the house was a happy one, full of laughter and love.

* * * * *

LARGER-PRINT BOOKS!

GET 2 FREE
LARGER-PRINT NOVELS
PLUS 2 FREE
MYSTERY GIFTS

Love Inspired®
SUSPENSE
RIVETING INSPIRATIONAL ROMANCE

Larger-print novels are now available...

YES! Please send me 2 FREE LARGER-PRINT Love Inspired® Suspense novels and my 2 FREE mystery gifts (gifts are worth about $10). After receiving them, if I don't wish to receive any more books, I can return the shipping statement marked "cancel." If I don't cancel, I will receive 4 brand-new novels every month and be billed just $5.24 per book in the U.S. or $5.74 per book in Canada. That's a savings of at least 23% off the cover price. It's quite a bargain! Shipping and handling is just 50¢ per book in the U.S. and 75¢ per book in Canada.* I understand that accepting the 2 free books and gifts places me under no obligation to buy anything. I can always return a shipment and cancel at any time. Even if I never buy another book, the two free books and gifts are mine to keep forever.

110/310 IDN F5CC

Name	(PLEASE PRINT)	
Address		Apt. #
City	State/Prov.	Zip/Postal Code

Signature (if under 18, a parent or guardian must sign)

Mail to the **Harlequin®** Reader Service:
IN U.S.A.: P.O. Box 1867, Buffalo, NY 14240-1867
IN CANADA: P.O. Box 609, Fort Erie, Ontario L2A 5X3

**Are you a current subscriber to Love Inspired Suspense books
and want to receive the larger-print edition?
Call 1-800-873-8635 or visit www.ReaderService.com.**

* Terms and prices subject to change without notice. Prices do not include applicable taxes. Sales tax applicable in N.Y. Canadian residents will be charged applicable taxes. Offer not valid in Quebec. This offer is limited to one order per household. Not valid for current subscribers to Love Inspired Suspense larger-print books. All orders subject to credit approval. Credit or debit balances in a customer's account(s) may be offset by any other outstanding balance owed by or to the customer. Please allow 4 to 6 weeks for delivery. Offer available while quantities last.

Your Privacy—The Harlequin® Reader Service is committed to protecting your privacy. Our Privacy Policy is available online at www.ReaderService.com or upon request from the Harlequin Reader Service.

We make a portion of our mailing list available to reputable third parties that offer products we believe may interest you. If you prefer that we not exchange your name with third parties, or if you wish to clarify or modify your communication preferences, please visit us at www.ReaderService.com/consumerschoice or write to us at Harlequin Reader Service Preference Service, P.O. Box 9062, Buffalo, NY 14269. Include your complete name and address.

LISLPDIRI 3R

ReaderService.com

Manage your account online!

- Review your order history
- Manage your payments
- Update your address

> ### *We've designed the Harlequin® Reader Service website just for you.*

Enjoy all the features!

- Reader excerpts from any series
- Respond to mailings and special monthly offers
- Discover new series available to you
- Browse the Bonus Bucks catalog
- Share your feedback

Visit us at:
ReaderService.com

RS13